AGANST THE CLOCK

A DCI HARRY MCNEIL NOVEL

JOHN CARSON

DCI SEAN BRACKEN SERIES

DI FRANK MILLER SERIES

SCOTT MARSHALL SERIES

Old Habits

AGAINST THE CLOCK

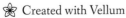 Created with Vellum

In memory of my friend, Clifton Bodiford

ONE

Lenny Smith stood at the exit door of the block of flats and put a hand on his side. He was sweating and had a stitch and that was just from coming down in the lift.

Down in the lobby, he'd stood and got his breath back. He double-checked that he had indeed removed his slippers and was pleased to see the trainers with the Velcro fasteners were on his feet.

He wasn't built for running. Not on a treadmill, and certainly not in the dark in the street where all the nightcrawlers were on the prowl.

But his doctor had strongly suggested he start exercising. So here he was, standing outside the doors of the tower block, finishing a cigarette, waiting for Fat Sam.

He remembered back in the day when Fat Sam's was a restaurant up at Fountainbridge, but now that it was gone, the only Fat Sam he knew was his mucker.

Five minutes later, his pal came out the doors, leaning on his walking stick. And it wasn't the one he used for his disability interviews, but a nice carved wooden one.

The sun was coming up now, and Sam thought the same way as Lenny: no sense in going out in the dark and inviting the muggers.

Now Sam was finally here. 'Morning, cock,' he said, smiling. 'Ready for a jog along the promenade?'

'No.' Lenny looked at his watch. 'Six o'clock on a Saturday morning and you're smiling? There's a want about you, pal.'

Sam laughed. 'Cheer up, neighbour. I don't know about you, but I want to see seventy.'

'Christ, I'm only sixty-two, Sammy. And you're only a hair away from sixty-one. We're hardly near seventy.'

'That's the point. We don't want to be dropping dead before retirement age.'

'We don't work,' Lenny said.

'Exactly. Come on, let's get this show on the road.'

For April, it was sunny, but there was yet any warmth to be felt. Later on maybe, but right now the wind was whipping off the sea and making Lenny shiver. Still, once they upped the pace, he would feel sweat running down his legs. At least he always hoped it was sweat.

They turned left at the bottom of the hill, making for the traffic island. They would get to the middle of the road and make sure there was nothing coming before crossing the other half.

'Wee bastard on one of them dirt bikes nearly got me the other day,' Sam said as they crossed the first lane and stood in the relative safety of the island. 'Came roaring along that road from Portobello like he had just stolen the fucking thing. Which he probably had. He was more than likely on his way to burn it out somewhere. Beats paying for a taxi, I suppose.'

'Just keep concentrating, Sammy,' Lenny said, feeling his shirt sticking to him already.

They saw a white-and-madder double-decker coming towards them, and Lenny knew some of these bus drivers were mad bastards.

'Hurry! Run!' he shouted, but neither of them ran. They wobbled and hobbled, but made it in one piece while the big bus went flashing by, almost parting Lenny's hair in the middle.

'These big buses nowadays,' Sam complained. 'They go like a rocket, and sometimes I swear Stirling Moss is driving one.'

'Rest his soul.'

'Aye. Legend.'

They walked past the Chinese where they got their

Saturday night takeaway when the four of them got together for scran and a few beers.

'Still on for tonight, pal?' Lenny said, nodding to the closed restaurant.

'Aye. Try and stop me. I've been in every night this week, listening to Cathy rumble on and watching Netflix. Time for a wee swally.'

There was a brief respite from the wind at this point, the building giving them shelter.

'You been along to the Wee Green Van this week?' Sam asked.

This was a little classic Citroen van, painted bright green, that served food and drinks down on the promenade.

'Aye. I had a coffee and a baguette. Before lunch. I made Jimmy, the owner, promise he wouldn't mention me being there if he saw me and the wife out having a stroll.'

Now they turned onto the promenade itself. The sea looked a wee bit choppy. Their pace wasn't a full-on jog but at least it was faster than a walk.

Lenny could feel the sweat starting already. He stopped, putting two fingers on his wrist to see if he still had a pulse. He puffed out a breath into the cool morning.

'Hold on, pal,' Sam said. 'My shoelace is out. These

bloody trainers are trying to kill me. The damn laces come out all the time.'

Sam had a look around, worried that somebody from the social might be gawking at them from the comfort of a wee white van, and leaned against a lamp-post with one foot on the sea wall.

'Keep a lookout, pal,' he said, exaggerating his movements.

Lenny sat down on the wall and looked back along the way they had come, at the beach and the cold sea dissipating on the sand. At the litter some ignorant bastard had left behind.

'The fuck is that?' Lenny said, getting up quickly, while not quite moving like his arse was on fire.

'What?' Sammy looked around as if expecting to see some snooper from the social with a camera pointing towards them.

'There, down on the beach. Somebody's dumped something.'

Lenny was leaning over the wall more now, trying not to take a heider onto the sand. 'Hold my hand.'

'So I will.'

'There's something big down there.' He straightened up, looking at his friend. 'Something wrapped in plastic. Like a big haul o' drugs or something.'

'Jesus. What if it is? I'm not touching it.

'What if it's some kind of treasure?' Lenny was moving back along the way they had come.

'Hang fire there, pal,' Sam said, following his friend but not at such a fast pace, although Lenny's walking speed wouldn't win him any gold medals.

Lenny stood at the end of the promenade waiting for his friend. 'Looks like something wrapped in shrink film, but not the kind you've got in your kitchen. Like the stuff that pallets of boxes are wrapped with.'

'I can see that,' Sam said, looking down onto the beach, sweat lining his forehead.

'Why are you sweating? You've got "benefits cheat" written all over you.'

'Away ye go. Although I thought I saw somebody with a suspicious bag walk by.' He looked at Lenny. 'Like he had a camera peeping through a hole.'

'You're the only one who peeps through fucking holes.'

'Are we going to have a closer look?'

'Aye. Come on.'

They walked down the ramp towards the sand and the sea, although the water was nowhere near this package that may or may not be about to change their lives.

'Christ, what do you think it is?' Lenny said.

It was cylindrical in shape, about six feet long, bulging in places.

'Poke it with your stick,' Lenny told his friend, giving him a gentle shove on the back.

'I'll poke you in a minute.' Sam wiped the sweat from his upper lip.

'Jesus. Roll it over. Maybe it'll have a label on it. It might have fallen off a ship. Something that's valuable, other than drugs.'

'You and your bloody drugs. You wouldn't know what to do with them.'

'Aye, that's true. Just help me roll it over.'

'No chance. Somebody could be watching.'

'Sake. Let me get it.' Lenny got a foot under it and managed to lift it a little bit, but it was too heavy to lift with his leg alone. He took his foot out, reached down, put both hands under it and lifted, rolling it over.

'Jesus Christ,' he said, jumping back.

At the top of the package, a face with dead, staring eyes looked out at them.

'Call the polis,' Lenny said, but Sam had already turned away and was throwing up his breakfast onto the sand.

'From the phone box on the main road,' Sam said when he was finished. 'I'm not getting involved.'

'Bit late for that, pal. But see that fake Irish accent you put on when we're making prank calls?'

'Aye.'

'Use that one.'

TWO

'Look, don't take this the wrong way, but have you put on weight?' Detective Chief Inspector Harry McNeil looked at his wife, who was seven months pregnant.

Detective Sergeant Alex Maxwell was standing looking out of their living room window. 'I had a dream last night that I was eating a giant marshmallow. If you find a pillow missing, I've got it up my dress.'

He grinned and smiled at her and her baby bump. 'That's swell.'

'Oh, shut up, McNeil. I've heard all your jokes. And so has Amy.' She ran a hand over her stomach and drank from a cup of green tea that tasted like sewage. She looked at her husband. 'I'm bored being at home, Harry. Take me with you.'

Harry was putting his Apple watch on. 'As much as I'd love to, sweetheart, you have to rest. Doctor's orders, remember? That's why you're on maternity leave.'

'What does he know? It's too early for maternity leave. I could have gone another month. Six weeks maybe. Hell, I could have given birth at my desk.'

'If we hadn't had that wee scare, then I would agree with you, but young Amy there is busy playing about with your insides and now you have to rest.'

'Jesus. Make it sound like a horror movie.'

He laughed. 'What are your plans for today?' He pulled his jacket off the back of one of their dining chairs and slipped it on, patting his pockets for his car keys.

'Oh, maybe go for a spa day, then have lunch with the Queen. My diary's quite packed.'

He stood looking at her.

She gave a sad smile. 'Sorry. I'm going to struggle down the stairs and toddle along to the supermarket.'

'We're up three flights. Please be careful.' He looked at her, waiting for her to confirm that she would indeed be looking after herself.

'I will. You go and enjoy yourself on the beach with your friends.'

'Hardly a day out when there's a body down there. And on a Saturday morning too. I was going to take you out for a wee drive, but maybe later. Or tomorrow.'

She held on to the mug with both hands. 'That would be nice.'

She turned away from him, looking out the window again, at the bowling club where her husband had been having a few drinks the night before, without her. She had made him go out for a few. No point in them both missing out on a relaxing Friday night, and God knew he needed a break from her, what with all the moaning she'd been doing recently, and shouting and cursing...

She realised he had left, vaguely remembering him saying goodbye, telling her he loved her. There were tears running down her face and she didn't know where they had come from.

Alex watched Harry as he crossed over to her red Audi – his now, since she couldn't drive. *Theirs*, now they were married. She wanted to open the window, shout out, *I love you!* But she stood there looking down at him instead.

Then the little red car was away and she was left alone once again. She'd thought they would try to do something fun this weekend, but the anonymous phone call to the police had put paid to their plans.

Chance, her stepson, would be coming to stay tomorrow; he was on a week's leave from duties as a uniformed constable in Glasgow. She was looking forward to seeing him again.

Everything was going right in her life except for a couple of small things: her parents still didn't want anything to do with her because she'd married Harry, even though she was going to have their grandchild, and she was convinced her husband was going to leave her for the new DS he was partnered with. Lillian O'Shea. A red-haired Irish leprechaun. Although her hair wasn't flame red or anything. And she was considerably bigger than a leprechaun. But she was young, smiled a lot and had a better personality than Alex had these days.

'You're a silly wee besom, Alex Maxwell,' she chided herself. She was officially Alex McNeil now but had kept her maiden name for work, and it was still strange to think of herself as matriarch of the McNeil clan.

She put her cup away in the kitchen and looked for a jacket. Nothing too light and nothing too heavy. Spring was round the corner but hadn't sprung yet. No doubt she'd be sweating like a French hoor by the time she got down the stairs but then freezing her tits off when she got outside.

The doc had told her to be active, and Harry seemed to think that this meant sexually active, but she had told him that it was more of a twice round the block sort of deal, not knickers off twice a night.

She loved Harry so much and she would try for

him, but sex was the last thing on her mind right now. Lillian O'Shea was the newest member of their team, supposedly on temporary maternity leave cover, and though she trusted Harry, there was always temptation put in the way. She hoped Lillian wasn't going to be a temptation for Harry.

Everything was changing. Alex's colleagues. Her life. Her body. She just hoped that change wouldn't touch her husband. She wanted him just the same as he was. Life changed, she knew that, but it was changing at a pace she couldn't keep up with.

She grabbed a jacket that was warm but wouldn't look like a tent on her. She looked at the small table in the hall, expecting to see her car keys there, then remembered Harry had taken them.

He had gone to pick up Lillian. They were carpooling today. 'It's on the way,' he had said after giving her a call. Not just on the way but round the fucking corner. What were the chances of the Irish cow living round the corner from them? She had been stationed at Gayfield station before transferring down here.

Alex had met her once. 'I lucked out getting seconded to MIT at Fettes,' Lillian had said.

That was an understatement. Fettes was Harry and Alex's station, just round the corner from where they lived.

Alex could feel tears burning her eyes. It wasn't fair. She was carrying Harry's child, and now he was out fucking about with some Irish bint who was younger than her. Better looking. Better smile. Fitter. Bigger tits. But not a bigger belly. Oh no, Alex was well ahead in that one. Lillian wasn't fucking pregnant. Yet.

Alex grabbed her house keys and opened the front door, just as their neighbour across the landing, Mia, was coming up the final flight of stairs with two bags of shopping.

'Hello, Alex,' Mia said, smiling. 'Going out? Well, duh, of course you're going out. What gave it away, eh? Stupid cow that I am.'

Alex looked at her friend and neighbour and didn't know what to say. So she just started crying instead.

'Oh, come on, love, come in for a cuppa,' Mia said as she put her grocery bags down.

Alex nodded and pulled her own door closed behind her. Mia unlocked her front door and Sylvester, her cat, came running out and rubbed himself round Alex's legs. Then he scooted back inside, sensing there might be a treat for him, but not if he stood here arsing about.

Mia picked up her bags and the two women went inside.

THREE

DS Lillian O'Shea was waiting at the bottom of her street for Harry. Comely Bank Row was literally round the corner from Harry's flat in Comely Bank Terrace. She was dressed in black jeans and a black leather jacket. The red hair stuck out, if not quite like a fire engine then certainly in the region of a Lothian bus. Harry wondered if it was natural or out of a bottle. Surely somebody wouldn't dye their hair that colour on purpose?

'Morning, sir,' Lillian said, getting into the passenger side.

'Morning, Lillian,' he said. 'Nice day for a drive down to the beach.' He full-named her, not wanting to call her by the shortened version she had told him to use if he wanted. Lil. He didn't like that. It made her sound like she was trying to come up with her rapper name and could only think of half. Lil what? Lil Irish Girl? Lil Big Mouth? Lillian he was comfortable with; Lil was crossing the line. For him anyway. DI Ronnie Vallance seemed to have no problem with it.

'It would be a nice trip to the beach if there wasn't a dead girl on it,' she said, her Irish lilt heavy and pronounced.

'Aye. Doesn't do much to promote the area right enough.' He pulled away from the kerb.

'Was she washed up on the shore?' Lillian asked as he headed through Stockbridge's Raeburn Place.

'Not as far as they can tell. She was up from the shoreline.' And then he started playing 'Stranger on the Shore' by Acker Bilk in his head again. Christ, it would be there all day now. Should he put the radio on, try to get another tune in his head, or just ride it out, hoping it would fade?

Where the hell had he heard Acker Bilk anyway? Maybe Alex had had the radio on or something, tuned into some obscure station. She'd been doing weird things recently and listening to Acker Bilk was probably one of them. Not that Acker Bilk was weird, but Alex listening to his music definitely was.

'"Bird of Paradise" by Snowy White,' he said.

'What's that, sir?' Lillian asked.

He realised he'd spoken out loud. 'You ever heard of it? The song, "Bird of Paradise"?'

'Can't say that I have.'

'I've got it stuck in my head,' he lied, wishing it *was* stuck there. The sax was still playing in his head. *Damn you, Acker.*

They headed through the New Town, along London Road, heading east.

'How you liking MIT?' Harry asked her, after they'd had a quick debate on Genesis: Peter Gabriel or Phil Collins? Lillian had earlier admitted to listening to 80s music and Genesis was up there on one of her Spotify playlists. Phil Collins, she'd said, and told him not to get her started on Marillion and Fish.

'I love it. It's what I've been heading for.'

MIT Harry realised, not Genesis.

'Jeni Bridge highly recommended you,' he said.

'Did she? That's fantastic. She's a great leader.'

Harry noticed Lillian's face had turned red. Not quite the same shade as her hair but not a dodgem car's ride away from it either.

'Second week in MIT and we get a shout for a body on the beach. This is your big chance to shine. It's not always like this.'

'I'll grab it by the balls,' she said, then slapped a hand over her mouth. 'Christ, sorry, sir. I meant I'd grab the opportunity by...' She was lost for a second. 'By the armpit.'

She groaned and her face turned up the heat.

Harry reckoned they could have started a campfire with it if they'd been camping.

'Well, whatever part of its anatomy you're going to grab, this opportunity has fallen into your lap. You're an experienced detective, but you'll get all the help you need or want. One thing about this job: you never stop learning. Just when you think you've seen it all, something will sneak up behind you and kick you in...the armpit.'

She laughed. 'I won't be afraid to ask.'

The sun was up and the traffic was light. They talked more music: Elvis and Michael Jackson conspiracy theories. Oasis or Blur? Lillian looked at him then.

'When's the last time you were in a pub and a Blur song came on and everybody started singing it?' she asked. 'Exactly. I was in a pub last night and they started playing "Wonderwall" and every bugger in the place was singing it.'

The Beetles versus the Stones was just starting to get heated when Harry pulled in behind one of the patrol cars.

The wind coming in off the sea caught him off guard for a moment. Had his hair been longer, he was sure it would have been blown into some kind of bouffant.

They showed their warrant cards to a uniform

standing next to the police tape that was barring entry to the promenade at this end.

Down on the sand, a big bastard in a wax jacket was standing with his hands in his jacket pockets. His hair was being pulled over his head in a comb-over, although DI Ronnie Vallance wasn't going bald. He was tall as well as broad, and if anybody ever needed plans to build a brick shithouse, then a photo of Vallance would do the trick.

'What's the script here, Ronnie?' Harry asked, trudging across the sand to where Vallance was standing with DS Eve Bell.

'Morning, sir. Lil.' Vallance pointed to the phone box up on the pavement. 'Anonymous phone call made from that call box up there. Male voice, Irish accent, but it sounded put on. Not like yours.' He nodded to the DS.

'How could they tell?' Lillian asked.

'It just sounded fake, by all accounts,' Vallance replied. 'The treble-nine operator thought it sounded like a wind-up at first. It was only taken seriously when a patrol unit was dispatched and they found that lassie there.'

They turned to look at a forensics tent that had been erected close to the sea wall. Harry assumed that the 'lassie there' was still inside, being processed.

'Any ID on her?' Lillian asked.

'Aye. Kate Murphy will give you the grand tour. She's in there now, poking and prodding the victim.'

Harry nodded and indicated for Lillian to follow him. He pulled open one of the flaps on the tent and saw the plastic-wrapped corpse at the feet of the pathologist. With Kate was Angie Patterson, one of the mortuary assistants. They both looked up as if an intruder had just come in, despite the beach being littered with more polis than used condoms.

'Harry,' Kate said. 'Come in and have a look. Hello, DS O'Shea.'

'Morning, ma'am.'

Harry nodded to Angie, who was standing at the foot of the shrink-wrapped corpse. Both pathology women were wearing their white suits. Harry felt his feet slipping into the sand and wished he had put boots on.

'This is a new one on me,' he said, crouching down to have a look at the young woman's face. It had pink patches on it. 'Carbon monoxide poisoning?'

'I would say so,' said Kate. 'I cut the shrink wrap down the middle to do a preliminary exam and we found old clothing. Forensics want you to take a look before they bag it.'

Harry and Lillian snapped on nitrile gloves and Harry gently pulled the layer of wrap to one side. The deceased was fully clothed in a hoody and jeans, but there was a dress shoved inside.

Angie held up a plastic evidence bag. 'They bagged this lot but left it for you to see,' she said.

Harry took it and looked into it without opening it. There was a photo of a young girl wearing the dress that was inside the plastic. The girl looked like the victim, but younger.

'Turn the bag round,' Kate said. 'There's a name on the back of the photo.'

Harry turned it round and looked, holding the photo tight against the plastic bag.

Sandra Robertson.

'It's unusual for somebody to dump a body like this,' Lillian said. 'Usually, they're wrapped in a carpet.'

'This guy wanted to keep all this stuff together,' Harry said. 'Plus, she would have been easier to carry when he was dumping her, and not quite as obvious as a carpet.'

'It also looks like she was partially strangled once, but the marks are faded, like she was maybe tortured at one time,' Kate said. 'Looks like with something soft, like a scarf.'

'Rough time of death?'

'A few weeks ago, I'd say. There's evidence of the body being stored in a freezer. Maybe he killed her, then kept her somewhere while he figured out what to do with her.'

'Okay, Kate, thanks for that. I'll have somebody come down to the mortuary when you do the post-mortem. Probably Gregg and Eve Bell.'

'No problem. But if you change your mind, you're more than welcome to join us.'

'Thanks, but I have a lot of work to catch up on.'

It was known just how much Harry hated attending the actual dissection of a victim. They were betting people in the mortuary and always had a book going for whenever Harry turned up, to see whether he would toss his bag or not. 'It's the smell,' he would tell them, but he'd still be open to mockery nonetheless.

He left the tent with Lillian and approached Vallance, who was talking with a uniformed sergeant. He was giving her some order. Harry saw Simon Gregg up on the promenade.

'He can't swim,' Vallance said, coming over to Harry with a stumbling gait as his shoes sank into the sand.

'The sea's nowhere near us,' Harry said. 'The big streak of piss better not be skiving. Is there a lassie up there he fancies or something?'

'He's trying to find any witnesses who maybe saw somebody using the phone box. One person thought he saw somebody in it, but he was having a piss in it last night.'

Phone boxes were disappearing all over Edinburgh as mobile phones made them redundant, but they were widely used as toilets by drunks going home at night. Harry didn't think somebody having a piss in a phone box was likely to have left a shrink-wrapped corpse standing up outside while he did the business.

'Right. Get the door-to-door started,' Harry said, looking up at the tower block across the road. 'And make sure they go in there. They have a good vantage point up there. Then we'll get back to the station and get the ball rolling. Sorry to spoil everybody's Saturday.'

'It's not like I have a life outside the station,' Lillian said, and Harry realised after a moment that she wasn't being sarcastic.

FOUR

'You want me to drive?' DS Robbie Evans asked his boss, DCI Jimmy Dunbar.

'*Drive* is hardly the fucking word I'd use to describe how you move a car from one place to another. Those big machines that take a wheelie bin up and down are called bin lorries. Look it up. They're a lot bigger than that arse piece you call a car.'

'I've had the brakes done on her.'

'*Now* you've had the fucking brakes done. That didn't help me when I nearly pissed myself after you had a blackout. That scaffie you nearly melted was glad he had black trousers on.'

'I was reflecting.' Evans unlocked the doors to their pool car and stood at the driver's side, holding the car keys out in case Dunbar wanted to take over.

Dunbar made a face, shook his head and got in the

passenger side. 'Reflecting?' he said when Evans climbed in. 'What were you reflecting on? How your hair's going thin on top?'

'It's not going thin. Is it?' Evans looked into the rear-view mirror and ran a hand over his head.

'It is. When I'm walking behind you outside in the sun, I have to wear sunglasses.'

Evans looked at Dunbar. 'Just because you wear a toupee.' He started the car and pulled out of the car park at the back of Helen Street station, where they were based.

'Toupee? Cheeky bastard. I go to a nice wee lassie near us who cuts my hair. She always tells me what a fine head of hair it is too.'

'And I suppose her guide dug brushes the floor after she's done.'

'You're only jealous, ya baldy wee bastard. Just wait till all you've got is a ring of white hair running round the sides of your heid. You'll be wishing you had hair like mine.'

'Aye right. When I get to your age, my hair will be long gone, I'll be having a piss at night without having to leave my bed and I'll take a wee blue pill to go out on a Saturday night.'

'Listen, son, me and Cathy are going out tonight and I will not be needing the aid of some chemicals. I was also out last night and had a fair kick o' the ball.

And here we are, Saturday morning, out on a job and my eyes are clear and shiny. Unlike yours. You look like you've been drinking hairspray again.'

'What do you mean, again? And how can you drink hairspray?'

'Spray it into a glass.'

'You seem to know how it works. Besides, I was out with Vern, having a few sociable drinks.'

They had met Vern a few months back in the run-up to New Year when they were working a job up in the Highlands. She and her security co-workers had come down to Glasgow to work.

'What about Muckle McInsh?' McInsh was ex-Glasgow polis, Dunbar's DI back in the day. Now he worked private security.

'I didn't see him or his radge dug.'

Dunbar whipped his head round to Evans. 'Sparky's a good dug. You're the radge.'

'I'm just saying. The last time I picked Vern up, Muckle was there and it took Sparky a second to make out who I was. I was sweating like a bastard. He doesn't listen to Muckle at times. It's like he's got a loose wire in his heid, and he starts growling and gnashing his teeth before his eyes get the message.'

'He's a good boy. Almost as good as my Scooby.'

'At least Scooby recognises me when I come round to yours.'

'Maybe I should teach him to bite your baws,' Dunbar said.

'Never happen. He likes me too much.'

'Aye, well, just you make sure you don't go messin' that poor lassie about, or else Muckle will pull your baws through the back of your heid.'

'Aye, he is a big bastard right enough.' Evans looked at Dunbar. 'Big, I mean. Not a bastard.'

'I know what you meant. I still have all my fucking marbles.'

Evans guided the car round a side road towards the abandoned leisure park.

'Fuck me sideways,' Dunbar said, 'there's Calvin Stewart's car. I was hoping he'd have been and gone by now.'

Detective Superintendent Calvin Stewart was Dunbar's boss and the man who had called him at home that morning, breaking the news that his peaceful weekend was about to be anything but.

The complex had fallen into disrepair years ago and looked like it from the outside. The only sign of life was the patrol cars and other emergency vehicles parked outside.

Evans parked behind a police van and then they caught sight of the DSup standing near an opening into the building.

'Talk of the Devil,' Dunbar said as Stewart clocked them.

'Where the fuck have you two been?' Stewart said by way of introduction as they walked over.

'You told us to meet you at the station, sir, but when we got there, the desk sergeant passed on your message to meet you here,' Dunbar said.

'That was fucking yonks ago.' Stewart looked at Evans. 'You out on the fucking pish last night?'

'I did have a few with Chief Inspector Dunbar, sir,' Evans lied.

'Oh, aye. Bumming around with each other after hours? You know what we used to call blokes like you two back in the day?'

Dunbar focused on his pension, his dog and his wife, and put his hands in his pockets just in case one of them landed on Stewart's chin.

'I hope it was *buddies*,' Dunbar replied. *For your fucking sake.*

'Aye, something like that. Anyway, can't stand around here fucking gabbing like a pair of old sweetie wives. That wee wank muffin is inside.'

Evans wanted to ask what wank muffin, there were so many of them going around, but let Dunbar ask the question.

'What wank muffin?' Dunbar said.

'That wee fucking teuchter. What's his name again? Fudboy O'Penis.'

'Finbar O'Toole,' Dunbar corrected, thinking of the head of forensics.

'Aye. The haggis-shaggin' wee bastard. He brought his blow-up sheep with him and now he's going about greetin' like a wee lassie 'cause it won't keep the air in. I can only assume that's the reason he raised his voice to me. I had to come out and get some fresh air before I planted my fucking boot right up his jacksie. When you see him in there, you might want to have a wee word wi' him about shortening his life span.'

'I'll see what I can do,' Dunbar said. Then, as Stewart turned away, he looked at Evans and said in a low voice, 'Why did you tell him you were out drinking with me?'

'It was better than explaining about Vern.'

'No, it fucking wasn't. Now he thinks we can't get enough of each other. Wee bastard.'

They followed their boss into the leisure centre, which resembled anything but at this point. Unless the new thing was to have guests slit their feet open on the broken glass littering the floor, or catch scabies or God knows what else in the derelict building.

'I thought they were going to pull this place down?' Evans said.

'It's going to cost over half a million to bulldoze this

pile of shite,' Stewart explained in a way that even the most non-technical person would understand.

'Richt, that's enough, ya big, clumsy arse,' a voice shouted over at them. Dunbar looked further along to see a white-suited man standing and looking at them.

Stewart turned to them. 'See? Mouthy wee bastard he is. Only been here a fucking week and already he's getting on my tits. I want you two to be witnesses that he took a swing at me if I lamp the wee wanker. Fucking talking to me like that.'

'Did you hear me?' O'Toole shouted again.

'We're no' fucking deef!' Stewart bellowed. He reached a hand into his pocket and brought his lighter out. His lucky one. His therapist said he needed to keep a soft rubber ball in his pocket so at times like these he could squeeze it, but what the fuck did he know?

'There's no smoking in here,' O'Toole said. 'Obviously.'

'Did I say lamp him one?' Stewart said. 'I'm going to set fire to the bastard in a minute.'

Dunbar stepped forward. 'Show us the deceased,' he said to O'Toole.

A skylight at the top of the roof, where the water slides started, provided some light around the main pool area. Small generators hummed in the background, powering arc lights.

'I told him not to touch anything, but he started poking at things,' O'Toole complained when they were out of Stewart's earshot.

The walls were graffitied. Others had been kicked through. Wires were hanging down in places where vandals had been looking for copper wires. A chair was stuck halfway through a wire-mesh window, its legs poking into the air, like a photo that somebody with a high-speed camera had snapped of it in mid-flight. Pink lockers were stacked up against the wall opposite the pool, their doors open.

'Fucking smell that pish,' Stewart said. 'And that's just him,' he added, nodding to O'Toole. His voice carried in the open air.

'I'm not paid enough to listen to him,' O'Toole said to Dunbar.

'Just take us to where she was found,' Dunbar said, leading the man away.

'Through here,' O'Toole said, taking Dunbar into a first-aid room. Paperwork was scattered all around the floor and an examination table was in place, but the only patient was a body wrapped in cling film.

'It's the stuff you would use to wrap a pallet,' O'Toole said. 'The pathologist will be back in a minute. I opened up the plastic and found several items of clothing in there with her. An old dress, underwear, polo shirt. Sizes that seem too small for her.'

'Jimmy Dunbar, as I live and breathe!' a big man shouted from behind.

Professor Duncan 'Disorderly' Mackay stood framed in the doorway of the small room. He was so big, it looked like he was struggling to squeeze himself in.

'Dunky. How are you this morning?' Dunbar asked.

'I've been so busy that I can't keep up with you. I told you to send me enough work to keep me in a job, no' have me run off my feet. How's a man supposed to fit in binge drinking when there's all this work to do? What say you, Toolie boy?'

O'Toole turned to look at the pathologist. 'I'm with you on that one, big man.'

Mackay gave out a loud laugh. 'We'll need to take Toolie to the polis club and get him blootered one night.'

'Aye, we'll do that,' Dunbar answered.

Then Mackay moved out of the doorway, the smile dropping from his face. Back to business. 'This is a bastard, Jimmy. Poor wee lassie. Looks like carbon monoxide poisoning was the cause of death. I'll get a better look at her when I get her on my table. It's anybody's guess if she was sexually assaulted or not, but there are faint ligature marks on her wrists, like she had been restrained, maybe a long time ago.'

Dunbar looked at the pink patches on the girl's neck and face. 'Any guess at time of death?' he asked.

'Weeks ago. It looks like she was preserved, like frozen, before being wrapped up like this.'

'Identification?' Dunbar asked O'Toole.

O'Toole looked across at Mackay before looking at Dunbar.

'Alice Brent.'

'Aye,' Stewart said from the doorway. 'Alice Brent. She went missing from this shithole five years ago. Only it was open back then. The place was filled with kids. And fucking paedos, no doubt.' He looked at O'Toole as he emphasised the last bit.

Dunbar looked at Stewart. 'She was taken from here and nobody saw anything. I remember the case.'

'You and that DI of yours, McInsh, ran the case. It was his last before he fucked off.' Stewart stepped into the room and Dunbar was glad to see he'd put his lighter away.

'Jimmy, I want you and Heid-the-Baw there to go through to Edinburgh. Your DI, Tom Barclay, can run things from here. He can ask McInsh about the case and you can liaise with him.'

'Edinburgh, sir?' Dunbar asked.

'Aye. They got one too. Wrapped up like Alice. She went missing five years ago. And they just got her back.'

FIVE

Harry was sitting at a computer in the incident room when DI Frank Miller walked in. He got up and walked over to his friend.

'Hey, Frank. How's things?'

'Fine. The kids are getting bigger every day. How's Chance?'

'Coming through for a week. He's got some time off, so he wants to spend it with his girlfriend-not-girl-friend. He tries to tell his old man that a man can be friends with a woman.'

DS Eve Bell looked over at them. 'They can. And I make no apology for eavesdropping. I've already spoken to Chance and given him the benefit of my wisdom.'

'When did you speak to my son?'

'Never mind that, sir. Just know that I'm a mother and will be keeping my own son straight.'

'So you were practising on my boy?'

'Correct.'

Miller laughed. 'I'm sure he knows what he's doing.'

'We'll talk about this later, DS Bell,' said Harry. 'Meantime, can you all gather round.' The other detectives turned in their chairs to look at the two men. 'I've asked DI Miller along here today to give us the rundown on Sandra Robertson. Our colleagues from Glasgow are coming through as well. You've worked with them before and they'll explain why they're joining us on this investigation.'

'Maybe we should wait until DCI Dunbar gets here,' Miller suggested.

'Aye. Good. I was going to suggest that.'

The others turned back to what they were doing and Harry chatted with Miller about love, life and the pursuit of happiness.

Twenty minutes later, Jimmy Dunbar and Robbie Evans walked in. They shook hands with Miller.

'Good to see you again, Harry,' Dunbar said.

'Have you seen Chance recently?' Harry asked.

'Aye. Five minutes ago. I knew he was having time off and coming through here, so we gave him a lift. We dropped him off at your place.'

'Brilliant. Cheers for that.'

'He said he would buy a round at the pub tonight. I told him, don't be daft, your dad'll buy us drinks.'

'I think I should teach my laddie the art of buying a round of drinks for his old man,' Harry said.

'Fight amongst yourselves, mucker. I don't care who's paying. Even young Robbie wants to get wired into paying for the booze. Eh, son?'

'Sorry, no speaky Eengleesh.'

'I bet you'll learn quickly when your car's on fire.' Dunbar looked at Miller. 'You coming along for a wee sesh tonight, son?'

'Thanks, but I'm going out with the wife. We're having a date night and managed to get a babysitter. I'll catch up with you later. I'm assuming you'll be around for a wee while?'

'Aye. Until we catch the bastard who did this.'

'Right,' said Harry, 'let's see what we have and Frank can give us a rundown on their background.'

They walked over to the whiteboard, where photos of the victim from the beach that morning were held on with magnets.

'Right, folks, we'll get a brief background from DI Miller first, then we'll go over what happened this morning. Then DCI Dunbar can pitch in with the Glasgow end. Frank, if you'd like to take centre-stage.'

Harry stepped aside so that Miller was facing the rest of the team.

'I worked this case almost five years ago, back in twenty-sixteen. DCI McNeil was with Professional Standards at the time, so he wasn't working cases.' Miller looked around the room to make sure everyone was focused on him.

'It was a missing person's report that kicked it all off. Sandra Robertson's parents called the police when she didn't come home after school. It was a week before school broke up for the summer holidays. Sandra was in her last year at North Merchiston Primary School. Her parents live in Merchiston.'

'Where was she reported missing from?' DI Ronnie Vallance asked.

'She went down to Portobello Beach with some friends to the amusement arcade there. According to her best friend, the four of them stuck together except for when Sandra left the arcade to use the bathroom outside. There are two public toilets just off the promenade and she was going there. She was last seen talking to two boys from school. Apparently, a few of them from the school were there that night and they knew Sandra. They said she headed towards the toilets, and that was the last anybody saw of her.'

'What about her phone?' Robbie Evans asked.

Miller looked at him. 'The records were handed

over by the phone company and there weren't any unusual numbers there. It was all her pals and they all checked out. It stopped pinging at Portobello Beach, so whoever took her got her phone from her pretty quickly and switched it off. Forensics have it now and they'll see if they can get it going, and we'll get the phone company to look at the number again. Her parents never stopped paying the bill, so the number is still assigned to Sandra's phone. It's her original iPhone Five.'

'How old was she when she went missing?' Eve Bell asked.

'Twelve,' Miller answered. 'The night she went missing she was told by her parents to be home before dark, so she wasn't supposed to be out late. Her parents admit they're a bit overprotective and they started calling the parents of the friends she was out with. The friends were home and said they thought Sandra had gone off with the boys.'

'Is that something she would normally do?' Lillian asked.

'Not according to her parents. She never got into trouble, either at school or outside. She was an outgoing girl but not stupid.'

'Maybe she knew her abductor,' DI Karen Shiels said. 'Somebody she trusted who could get her to walk away with him.'

'Possibly. There were no reports of any girl screaming or struggling around that time or any time that evening. Knowing her abductor is an avenue we explored at the time, but we didn't come up with any viable suspects. It's like she vanished into thin air. There were no ransom demands and it went cold. She wasn't heard from again until she was found wrapped on the beach.'

'And now she's dead of carbon monoxide poisoning after five years?' Lillian asked.

Miller looked at her for a second before answering. 'Hold that thought. We were briefed before we came in here, and I'd like DCI Dunbar and DS Evans to give you a rundown on their victim first.' Miller stepped aside and all eyes were glued on the Glaswegian detectives.

SIX

Jimmy Dunbar looked grim as he stood in front of the team. 'Like you, we had a victim found today – at an abandoned leisure centre in Glasgow. Same cause of death. Then wrapped in industrial shrink wrap. There are indications that she was restrained, with ligature marks on her wrists, but not recently. The reason me and my colleague are through here today is, this girl also went missing five years ago. Her name was Alice Brent, and she disappeared without a trace from the leisure centre after she went there on a school trip from Edinburgh. They were going swimming there for the day.'

Evans stood to the side.

'Can I ask what the kids were doing in a swimming pool in Glasgow, sir?' Ronnie Vallance said.

Dunbar looked at Evans.

'We later discovered that one of the teachers was originally from Glasgow and thought it would be a nice day trip on the bus through to the centre. Just a wee change for the kids,' Evans said. 'The investigation was ours, obviously, as it happened on our patch, but we worked with DI Miller and his team because of the similarity in the cases. We were working on the theory they were linked.'

'And of course it would seem that way,' Dunbar said. 'Especially after the third abduction.'

'Zoe Harris was eight when she went missing,' Miller added. 'Also from Edinburgh. Abducted at the shows on the Links in Burntisland. She was there with her mum and dad and her little brother. It was a busy Friday evening and the kids were running about. The mother swore that Zoe was there one minute, and she took her eyes off her for a second and then boom, she was gone. She contacted the police, who searched the fairground, and the carnies even let them search their caravans, but nothing was ever found of little Zoe.'

'How close to the others, time wise, was she abducted?' Lillian asked.

Miller looked at her before answering. 'The same day as Alice.'

'And what time did Alice go missing?'

'Two thirty in the afternoon. Zoe, just after seven thirty that same night. Five hours between them going missing.'

Karen Shiels looked at Miller. 'Was a connection ever made back then?'

'They went to the same school. Zoe wasn't in the same class as Alice because she was two years younger than her, so they had different teachers, and the families didn't know each other, as far as was made out to us. Going to the shows in Burntisland was nothing new for them.'

'Lots of kids go missing every year,' Harry said. 'Then, unfortunately, it's sort of out of sight, out of mind. New cases come along and old ones are put on the back burner. It's a living hell for the parents, and they're the ones left behind.'

'The first victim found today was in a location where she was pretty much guaranteed to be found,' Lillian said. 'The one in Glasgow seems to be different. If it's the same killer – and let's face it, there's a good possibility it is – then how could he know Alice would be found?'

'Armadillos,' Dunbar said, and saw the confusion on Lillian's face. 'Perimeter Intruder Detection System. The building was getting vandalised, but it was more of a safety thing. These modules are on legs and have cameras, Wi-Fi, Bluetooth, all sorts of stuff fitted, and they're placed strategically near doors. When one detects an intruder, it sends a signal to the control centre run by the company that owns it. They can activate a high-decibel alarm, and they capture video. That's what happened today, just before sunrise. A hooded figure is seen walking into the building carrying the victim. It's not apparent what the object is from the video feed.'

'Was the door unlocked?' Eve Bell asked.

'It was thought to be locked, but there are that many YouTubers who film abandoned buildings, one of them could have broken the lock and sneaked in without the system going off. Or broken the lock after it was checked, just before the Armadillos were installed. Like some YouTuber knew they were going to be installed and wanted to get in and film before they became fully operational. We don't know exactly.'

Harry looked at Eve. 'Can you have a check on YouTube and see if you can find any videos of the place being filmed while it's abandoned?'

'I'll get right on that, sir,' she replied and turned to her computer.

Harry looked at Miller. 'If this guy did take Zoe Harris from Burntisland, and he's killed or been responsible for the deaths of Alice and Sandra, it's a safe bet that he'll leave Zoe in a place where she can be found.'

'It is. It's just a waiting game now, but I don't think we'll have to wait long.'

SEVEN

'How's Alex?' Jimmy Dunbar asked from the passenger seat of the Audi.

'Mood swings,' said Harry. 'Peeing five times a night. Doing a good Linda Blair impression at times. Life couldn't be better.'

'That's why I'm single,' Robbie Evans said from the back seat.

'Aye, that's why you're fucking single,' Dunbar said. 'Nothing to do with the fact your maw still washes your skids.'

'I'm a free bird. No woman is going to tie me down.'

Dunbar turned to look at him. 'Stop talking pish. You'd be lucky if a woman wanted to tie you down, and I don't mean on a Friday night when you're blootered.'

'I do like Vern, though. I could see myself being with her long term.'

Dunbar looked at Harry. 'Have you ever heard such slavering pish? One minute he's a gigolo, the next he's picking out a pair of slippers and a pipe. Make up your bloody mind.'

'Hey, I'm no gigolo. I have limits, you know.'

'I thought your limit was your maw's pals at the bingo? Anything above their age is a no-go, and that only rules out females with no pulse.'

'That's disgusting.'

'Linda Fry wasn't disgusting, though, eh? You were just keeping her pension book warm.'

'They're more your age, my mum's pals.'

'Cheeky bastard. I don't need to splash Old Spice down my fucking Ys to attract some old lush.'

Harry laughed.

'You hear him, Harry? This is the sort of bollocks I've got to listen to every day,' Dunbar said. He looked at Evans again. 'Tell Harry about the lipstick you were wearing a couple of weeks ago.'

Evans shook his head. 'I was working undercover. Some drag queens were being mugged. We stepped in.'

'It nearly gave me the fucking boak looking at him wearing a dress. And that was just on his day off.'

'Funny. We got him, though, didn't we?'

'We did. And the mugger got a good kick in the nanchucks thanks to Robbie.'

'Bastard put his hand up my dress. Well, I wasn't putting up with that. He hadn't even bought me a drink.'

'Bought you a drink...Jesus, listen to yourself. You should be so lucky.'

'At least you got the bastard,' Harry said. 'That kind of shite shouldn't be tolerated nowadays. Live and let live, eh, fellas?'

'Amen to that. Some bastards need taught a lesson, though. And that bloke got one that night. One of our undercover sergeants was dressed as a pro and she got a boot in at him too.'

Harry looked for a space in Bryson Road, but there weren't any, so he parked on double yellows and put the police sign in the windscreen. It was sunny but far from warm, with a chill wind blowing through.

'Flat number three,' he said, nodding to the stair door. 'He said he's going to be in.'

He was. They were buzzed in and made the climb up to the first floor, where a thin man was waiting for them. He looked older than his years. Harry had pulled the file before coming here and they had read the details of the family. Brian Robertson was forty-one, but his slippers and loose-fitting cardigan would have looked better in a retirement home. His hair was salt and pepper, with the emphasis on salt. His skin was waxy and pale.

'Come away in.' He held out his left arm, indicating which way they should go.

An open door led into the living room. They stood around waiting for him, none of them keeping their back to the door. The room was immaculate, with very few possessions on display, except for a photo of a young girl. Harry knew he was looking at the girl they had found that morning.

'Sit down,' Robertson said, shuffling into the room.

Harry and Dunbar sat on the couch like Jehovah's Witnesses who had actually made it through the front door and didn't know what to do now. Evans stood by the door, keeping an eye on the room and the hallway behind him.

'Can I make some tea or something?' Robertson asked, sitting down on the chair carefully, like it would explode if he plonked himself down.

'Is Mrs Robertson in?' Harry asked.

Robertson looked at him with wet eyes. 'She died. Six months ago.'

'Sorry to hear that.'

'Aye. I'm hanging on in case Sandra comes back.' He looked at each of them in turn, as if waiting for an affirmative, that it was a good idea to wait for his daughter to return.

'I'm sorry to have to tell you this,' said Harry, 'but we discovered a body this morning and we think it's Sandra.'

Robertson sat perfectly still but took in such a sharp breath that Harry thought the man was taking his last one. Then he spoke.

'Jesus. Please tell me it's a mistake.'

'I'm sorry,' Dunbar said, 'but we're sure.'

'Is it Sandra they're talking about on the radio? The body they found on the beach?' Robertson's voice was raspy now, like it belonged to an eighty year old.

'Yes, it is,' Harry replied.

'Did she drown?'

'No, it looks like she died of carbon monoxide poisoning.'

'Carbon monoxide? Like you get when a gas heater is faulty?'

'Yes,' Harry said. 'It would seem she was somewhere that had a leak and she died from it.'

Robertson looked into thin air for a moment. 'When did she die?'

'A few weeks ago,' Dunbar said.

Robertson's breathing became more laboured. 'So she's been alive all this time? Nobody murdered her. Stabbed her or cut her throat or anything like that. Somebody kept her, and then she died of poisoning?'

'Yes, we believe she'd been held somewhere all this

time,' Dunbar said. 'And now we need to ask you some questions. Starting with, where were you last night?'

Robertson's mouth opened and closed a few times before he answered. 'You can't think I did this? That I was responsible?'

'We just need to eliminate you from our enquiries, Mr Robertson,' Evans said.

And it was this comment that broke the camel's back. Robertson's face crumpled and he started sobbing, putting his face into his arms and crying uncontrollably.

Harry looked at Evans and made a phone gesture with his thumb and pinkie: *call for the family liaison officer.*

Evans nodded and left the room, finding the kitchen. They could hear his muffled voice talking to somebody as Robertson gathered himself.

'Is there anybody we can call to come be with you?' Harry asked.

Robertson nodded. 'Mike and Agnes. Morton. They're my friends.'

'Give me their number and I'll get DS Evans to call.'

Robertson rattled it off for Evans when he came back into the room, then he left once more.

'This is going to be hard, Mr Robertson, but we're here for you. You'll get all the help you need. First, though, we need to know where you were last night, so we can establish a timeline,' Dunbar said.

Robertson conceded the point and nodded. 'I was here. I work in Sainsbury's at Westfield during the day, and I come home at night and sit by the phone. Every night.'

Harry nodded. 'Can you tell us about anybody who you thought might have taken Sandra at the time,' he said. 'We read the file, but we want to see if there's anybody else you might have thought of since you made your statement.'

Robertson shook his head. 'No. I think she was in the wrong place at the wrong time. A pervert took her.'

Evans came back into the room and nodded to Harry. 'Mr and Mrs Morton will be over soon. They live out in Corstorphine, but they're on their way.'

'Was Sandra ever in trouble at school?' Dunbar asked.

Robertson shook his head. 'No. Never. She and her friends were good kids. The teachers loved them.'

'Did she ever go on a school trip to the Swim World leisure centre in Glasgow?'

Robertson looked blank for a moment, then his eyes widened a bit. 'Yes. She went there a week before she went missing. I remember because her mother and I argued over whether she should go or not. I was over-protective. See how that turned out, eh? Ironic, isn't it?

I was overprotective but couldn't protect her when the time came.'

'You can't blame yourself,' Harry said.

'Did she have a good time at Swim World?' Dunbar said, steering the conversation back on track.

'Yes. She had a good time. Her friends were there. It was a good day out for twelve year olds.'

'You remember how they got there?'

There was a knock at the door and Evans answered it. A woman rushed in, followed by two men.

'Oh, Brian. I am so sorry. I heard on the news, and when that policeman called, I just knew it was your baby. Oh God.' Agnes Morton leaned over and put her arms around Robertson, sobbing.

While she cried, the two men introduced themselves as Mike Morton and his brother-in-law, Marshall Mann. Harry introduced himself and his colleagues.

'I'm really sorry, mate,' Morton said to Robertson when his wife drew back. 'I can't believe it.'

'Me neither,' Mann said. He looked to be in his late thirties, with designer stubble and fashionable glasses.

Dunbar and Harry both stood up. 'I was asking how the girls got to Swim World,' Dunbar said.

Robertson had to think about it again. 'Yes. They went on a coach. Mike's coach.' He nodded to his friend. 'Walter Scott Travel. Mike owns the business and he gave the school a good price. Didn't you, Mike?'

The three policemen looked at him.

'Yes, I did,' Morton answered. 'The business was a lot smaller then, so I had to take what I could. I had to hunt for business, and back then I even had to tinker about with the engine. Different now, though. I've got a few private contracts for shuttle work, and we do private hire, as well as a couple of local service runs.'

'You were there when Alice Brent went missing,' Dunbar said.

'I remember you interviewing me at the time. I told you back then, I was sitting with some other bus drivers. I didn't know them, but it's like a solidarity movement when bus drivers get together. We were swapping war stories. I used to be an Edinburgh bus driver before I left and started my own business.'

'I checked the file again to refresh my memory and saw you had been cleared. All the drivers were sitting with each other in the café and you alibied each other. Then when it was time to leave, around the time Alice went missing, all the drivers were outside, chatting. There were no security cameras inside the building because of the issues of the changing rooms and lockers being near the pool. The only other camera was at the entrance. Alice was seen walking out ahead of her friends, and when they got outside, they thought she was on the bus. Turns out she wasn't and eventually we were called in.'

'That's right. And my bus was searched, which I was quite happy to let happen.'

Agnes Morton looked puzzled. 'I thought we were called here because Sandra had been found?'

'You were,' said Harry. 'I have a family liaison officer coming round, but if you could stay with Mr Robertson in the meantime, that would be great.'

'No problem,' she said, eyeing the policemen with suspicion.

The detectives left the flat.

EIGHT

Wee Shug gripped the top of the lower sash window and sneaked another quick glance down and thought he was going to puke. His legs were shaking, he was sweating like a Russian shot putter's bawbag and he was going to chuck his dinner over the window any minute.

It had to be at least a hundred and eighty feet to the ground, he told himself. At least. He thought about gobbing just to see if it would evaporate, but that would mean leaning out more than he was comfortable with, and besides, it might get on his new Nikes if he missed.

Instead, he turned to look through the window to the inside.

Where Muckle McInsh was standing watching him.

The big man inside shook his head and reached

over, sliding the top sash window down since Shug seemed to be standing on the lower one.

'Come on, ya fanny. Get inside,' Muckle said. Sparky was standing beside him, the German Shepherd panting and wagging his tail. Shug thought the dog was laughing at him.

'I can't. I'm stuck.'

'How are you stuck?'

'It's a hundred and eighty feet up here, and I'm frozen to the spot.'

Muckle shook his head. 'Don't talk pish. We're on the ground floor and that windowsill is barely three feet off the ground. Jump.'

'Jesus, don't talk like that. Fucking jump. You know how I hate heights.'

'Well, climb in then.'

'Help me, Muckle.'

'For God's sake.' Muckle stepped forward and grabbed hold of Shug's outstretched hand.

'Hurry, Muckle. I'm going to fall.'

Muckle pulled the small man through the top of the window, and Shug scrabbled his legs, and then he was in, falling through the air, sure he was going to meet certain death. He screamed as Muckle stepped back, and then he landed on the couch.

'What a bloody racket. Just as well the house is empty.'

'I wonder why he left this couch?' Shug said.

'I doubt that was his. Have you seen it? It's all fucking pish-stained. Looks like some junkie bastard couldn't be bothered going to the bog and let loose on it.'

Sparky put his two front legs on the couch and licked Shug's face.

'Get down, Sparky. You don't know what you'll catch. And the couch is minging too,' Muckle said.

'Very funny,' Shug said.

'What's all the noise?' Vern Baxter said, coming into the room.

'It's Shug. He went skydiving and landed on the couch.'

'On that pish-stained old thing? You're brave, Shug.'

Shug moved fast and was on his feet in a second. He looked back at the couch, which had some seriously dubious stains on the cushions. 'Christ, why didn't you tell me?'

'I did,' said Muckle. 'And you were only supposed to climb through the window, not stand on the sill looking like you were trying to tan the place.'

'I had to stand up there to try and get the window open. Get some leverage going. It was stiff.'

'Your heid's stiff. Next time, I'll take the window

and you can have the door. It was unlocked and we just walked in.'

'Fine by me.'

'No, wait. I'll have Sparky. Never mind.'

'Vern can come in through a window,' Shug said, grinning at Vern.

'Just when I thought you were a gentleman, you go and crush the dream,' Vern replied.

It was almost mid-afternoon and shadows were being thrown about the back garden by the tall trees, the same trees that gave them shelter from prying eyes.

'The house is empty,' Vern said. 'Except for that couch.'

'You should take that couch away with you, Shug, since you've bonded with it,' Muckle said.

'I wouldn't even put that bastard thing on a bonfire.' Shug looked around the room. 'So what now?'

'We're repo agents. When the suit went to repo Diamond Jim's Bentley, he was threatened. Diamond Jim isn't going to threaten us. Not twice anyway.'

'It seems that he's gone down in the world if all he's got is that crappy old Mini parked in front of the garage,' Shug said. It was an original one, smaller in size than the new ones.

'Oh, I think he's got more than a Mini,' Vern said.

'In the garage? You think he would walk away from this house, taking all his stuff, and leave a car worth well over a hundred grand just sitting in an abandoned garage?' Shug said.

Muckle raised his eyebrows.

'Right, I'm going outside to prove you wrong. I think we're wasting our time here.'

'Go ahead,' Muckle said to Shug's back as the small man walked out.

A few minutes later, Muckle walked out with Vern and Sparky to find Shug rocking the small car from side to side on its springs.

'What are you trying to do, Shug?' Muckle asked. Shug was merely a shadow behind the Mini.

'I'm going to roll it on its roof.'

'How the fuck are you going to manage that?'

'Like a woman can lift a car when her child's underneath it.'

Muckle bent down and gave an exaggerated look under the car. 'Nope, I don't see any child under there.'

'Funny. You two could give me a hand instead of standing there.'

Muckle looked at Vern and nodded, and then they both gave a round of applause.

'Bloody comedians.'

'We could help you roll it over, Shug, or we could just use these?' Muckle held up the car keys.

'You made me sweat first. I hope you both had a laugh watching me.'

'We did actually,' Vern said. 'The keys were on a hook in the kitchen.'

'Here, you're the short arse – get behind the wheel and move it. Then bring the keys back. There's one on there might open the garage,' Muckle said. Sparky thought he was about to throw a ball. 'Easy, ya hoor. If you swallow these, we'll have to wait twenty-four hours.'

Vern rubbed behind the dog's ear.

The small car's back bumper was pressed against the door, so there was no doubt the car had to be moved. Shug took the keys, got in and moved the car forward, then brought the keys back out.

He tossed them back to Muckle. 'Here, you're bigger than me. If somebody's going to come charging out, you and the boy there can have at it.'

'Deary me, you'll be first in line if there's a bonus, though, eh?'

'Goes without saying, mate.'

'Right then.' Muckle took a key and inserted it into the lock and swung the garage door open. And there was their prize, a nearly new Bentley Continental GT.

It was unlocked and the key fob was inside. Muckle got in behind the wheel.

'Right, boys and girls. Recovery fee will be ours tomorrow. Shug? Tell your husband to get the paperwork sorted. Tonight, we eat like kings.'

Sparky started barking and wanted in beside Muckle. 'Away, ya big furball. This car is going to keep you in dog meat for a while, so don't go ripping the fucking leather. Vern? Could you do the honours and take my boy?'

'My pleasure. Shug, you can drive while I sit in the back with my favourite boy.'

'I thought Robbie Evans was your favourite boy?' Shug said.

'He's my second favourite.'

Just then, Muckle's phone rang. 'Hi, Tom. What's up, pal?'

Muckle spoke to DI Tom Barclay for a couple of minutes before he hung up.

'What's that all about?' Vern asked.

'A wee girl went missing five years ago from Swim World. Now she's been found at the same place. Dead. Jimmy Dunbar is through in Edinburgh and his DI, Tom Barclay, wants me to go over the case with him since I worked it back then.'

'Oh God. Poor wee thing,' Vern said.

But Muckle didn't hear her. His mind had gone back to that time and place.

He couldn't wait to help Jimmy Dunbar again.

NINE

'I wonder what Frank Miller thinks of him,' Robbie Evans said as they got back in the car. 'Morton, I mean. Miller was the one who interviewed him back then.'

'His alibi was watertight, just like I said in there. The buses couldn't park right at the door, so they were in the car park at the back,' Dunbar said.

Harry started the car and pulled away from the side of the road. 'All those buses from different companies would leave at the same time?'

'Aye. So they were out there, gabbing. None of them left to be on their own. I just think he looks a creepy sod. If it wasn't for the alibi, I'd be all over him.' Dunbar sighed. 'One down, one to go. This is the part of the job I hate, telling a parent their bairn has been found dead.'

They drove round the corner and parked in Dorset

Place. In contrast to the last flat, this one was located in a modern building. It was blustery, the weather matching their moods. They climbed the three flights of stairs to the top flat and a woman answered Harry's knock. They showed their warrant cards and the woman's eyes widened.

'Is it about Alice?' she asked, her voice dry and raspy.

'It is. Can we come in?'

She walked away without answering and they followed her through to the living room, where a man was sitting watching football on the TV. He switched it off when they walked in.

'It's about Alice,' the woman said.

'Mr and Mrs Brent?' Dunbar asked.

They both nodded. Dunbar knew their names were Tim and Sheila.

'I'm from Glasgow Division, as is my colleague, DS Evans. We're helping DCI McNeil here with his enquiries into the disappearance of your daughter.'

'Was that her you found on Portobello Beach this morning?' Tim Brent asked, his eyes turning liquid.

'No, it wasn't,' Harry answered, and before he could carry on, Sheila Brent put a hand on her chest and let out a breath.

'Thank God.'

'I'm sorry, but it is bad news. That wasn't your

daughter, but Alice *was* found this morning. In the same location where she went missing.'

Sheila opened her mouth and seemed to lose the ability to breathe. They helped her down onto the settee.

Dunbar looked at Evans. 'Tea, Robbie.'

Evans left in search of a kitchen and a kettle.

They heard it being clicked on as Sheila gathered herself. She looked at the two detectives.

'How...how did she die? Did he hurt my baby?'

'It would seem that she died of carbon monoxide poisoning. We can't be a hundred per cent sure until a post-mortem is done, but that's the indication,' Harry said.

'Wait a minute,' Brent said, 'did she just die recently?'

'We think in the last few weeks,' Dunbar said, wishing that Evans would hurry up with the tea.

'Where has she been all this time?' Brent asked.

'We don't know,' said Harry. 'We just know that she was left back where she first went missing.'

'I was one of the investigating officers,' Dunbar said. 'I'm aware of the details surrounding your daughter's abduction, but we need to ask some more questions.'

Brent sat down beside his wife just as Evans came

through with the tea. Dunbar took the mug from him. 'Cheers, Robbie.'

Dunbar passed the cup over to Sheila and she drank from it, sipping the lukewarm liquid.

'I know it was five years ago, but since we first spoke to you have you remembered any little detail that you might not have remembered at the time?' Harry said.

Sheila looked at her husband like they were collectively thinking, and then they both looked blankly at the detectives.

'I can't think of anything. I mean, I've run the scenario through my head over and over,' Brent said. 'I mean, why would she wander off away from her friends? She was ten years old, for God's sake. She was so innocent.' His lips started to tremble. 'Who would want to take her?'

'That's what we're trying to find out,' Dunbar said.

'You couldn't find out five years ago,' Sheila said. 'What makes you think that you can find out now?'

'Two of the girls have been returned. We can learn things forensically. Try and work out where they were kept for five years.'

Brent looked at Dunbar. 'That other body from Porty; it was Sandra, wasn't it?'

'It was. Her next of kin have been informed. Did you know them at all?'

'No.' Sheila shook her head. 'I saw Sandra on the news when she went missing, down at Portobello, but we didn't know them personally.'

'What about Zoe Harris?'

'We heard about her too, of course – going missing on the same day as Alice. But the police officer, Frank Miller, didn't tell us much about the wee one. She went to the same school as Alice, but I don't ever remember seeing her when I took Alice. They were in different years. I might have seen her, but I don't remember.'

'Did Alice go on many trips?' Dunbar asked.

'A couple. They went through to the Glasgow Science Centre one time with her class. She had fun then.' She sipped her tea.

'How did they get there?'

'By coach. Two classes went that time, I think. Our Alice's class and Mrs Morton's.'

Dunbar looked at Harry before asking the next question. 'Mrs Morton? Do you know her first name?'

'It's Agnes,' said Brent. 'Her husband is the owner of the bus that took Alice through to Glasgow. And he's my boss. I'm a diesel mechanic.'

TEN

'Thanks for coming along,' DI Tom Barclay said to Muckle McInsh. Sparky wagged his tail.

'Nae bother, pal. If I can be of any help, that's the main thing. But let me introduce the team. Former sergeant Angus Kendal, a.k.a. Shug. Former DS Vern Baxter.'

Barclay nodded at them. 'Good to meet you all. Muckle has told me good things about you.'

'Has he?' Shug asked.

'No, not really. He said you were a shower of bastards.' Barclay looked at Shug's face before smiling. 'Just kidding. Come on, let me show you where the wee girl was found.'

Patrol vehicles were still parked in the car park in front of the abandoned leisure park.

'This has seen better days,' Shug said.

'Aye, it's been shut a few years. Vandals got in and wreaked havoc with it until the Armadillos were put up,' Barclay told them. 'Watch Sparky's paws in here. There's broken glass everywhere.'

'Whoa, what the fuck?' Finbar O'Toole said when they got inside, striding across to them. 'A fucking dug in here? You've got to be shitting me.'

'This is former DI Michael McInsh,' Barclay said.

'I don't give a flying fuck who he is. I've had enough of you lot pissing all over my crime scene today. Who said you could come in here anyway?'

'Oy!' a voice boomed behind O'Toole. The man's face fell. Clearly, he hadn't expected Calvin Stewart to still be on the premises. 'Shut your fuckin' haggis chute, ya bagpipe shaggin' wee bastard. I asked them to come here today. Unlike you, McInsh has spent a lot of time working in this city.'

'This is fucking unheard of. A dug at a crime scene.'

'Have you never seen a fuckin' polis dug up close? I can arrange for him to let that bastard loose on your fuckin' bawbag.'

'Radge,' Muckle whispered to Sparky, the code word for the Shepherd to start snarling and barking. He started pulling hard against his harness.

O'Toole jumped back, gasping. 'See what I mean?

It's oot o' control. It could fucking kill one o' us at any time. Michty me.'

'Michty me?' scoffed Stewart 'You think you're Oor Wullie's stunt double or something? Stop talking in tongues, ya wee fanny. Yer in Glasgow now, so you can leave that fucking twang behind. Now get oot the fuckin' way while the real men – and woman – get on with the job. And I want a fuckin' report on my desk by the end of the day. And by God, there'd better be some decent reading in there, nothing that looks like a page from the fuckin' Broons. Michty me, indeed. Now, get oot mah fuckin' face.'

'Aye well, make sure he doesn't pish on the crime scene.'

'He's well trained,' Muckle said. 'He'll no' pish anywhere.' He locked eyes with the forensics investigator for a second, hoping he would say something else so he could add to Stewart's rant, but the forensics man just turned on his heel and walked away.

Sparky was still barking at the man. 'Easy, ya hoor. You'll have me in that fucking swimming pool and there's no water in it.'

Sparky stopped barking and wagged his tail.

'I take it you don't like him, sir?' Muckle said, keeping Sparky on a tight leash now, to avoid the debris on the floor. The dog had stopped snarling.

'He got under my fuckin' skin the minute I clapped

eyes on him, Michael. And he just keeps rubbing me the wrong way.'

Stewart was the only person who called Muckle by his given name.

'Right, she was in here. The pathologist took her away. She's going to do a post-mortem today since it's urgent, then the wee lassie will be transported back to Edinburgh.'

'Where exactly was she?' Muckle asked.

'Lying on that table. This is the first-aid room, and all the stuff was left behind when this place closed down. This room is close to the entrance, so when he set the Armadillo off, he knew they would come in and have a scout around, and that this was one of the first places they would look.'

'No witnesses, I take it, on the day she went missing?' Shug asked.

'None,' Muckle answered. 'We asked for people to come forward and there were plenty of sightings, but nothing came to fruition. It wasn't her.'

'What was the weather like that day?' Vern asked.

'It was raining. I remember thinking that the kids looked like they hadn't got dry after being in the pool. Why?'

'I was trying to picture what people would be wearing. If somebody had an umbrella, it would have been easy for them to hide under it.'

'Aye, that's a good point,' Barclay said.

'Oh, that's a nice dog you've got there,' said one of the white-suited techs, standing at the doorway. Sparky wagged his tail at her. 'Can I clap him?'

'Sure.' Muckle loosened the leash a bit and the Shepherd went over to see her.

'How old is he?'

'Just turned three.'

'Oh, you're such a good boy. Yes, you are.' The girl laughed and walked away after rubbing Sparky's ears.

'The buses were parked at the far end of the car park,' Muckle said. 'The kids came out the front door and turned left, along the pavement, and they had to cross the road. Before that they were told to wait in line for the second class to come out. It was pelting down, one of the teachers said, and a few of the boys were acting up, clowning around, and there were other people going into the swimming pool, so in general there was a lot of confusion. It was only when they got on the bus and did a head count that they realised Alice Brent was missing.'

'We have to wonder why he took her and kept her alive for five years,' Barclay said. 'Usually, they're dead within forty-eight hours.'

'He obviously had this all planned out,' Shug said.

'Give us your thoughts, wee man,' Stewart said.

'There are a lot of people going about. Lines of kids

waiting to get on the bus. Adults with kids coming and going. Now, I know that could be a recipe for disaster; a child being snatched might draw attention. And Alice was ten and bigger than, say, a five year old, so she might have had the gumption to shout out if somebody grabbed her. There's a possibility, then, that she knew her abductor and went quietly.'

'All the bus drivers and teachers were vetted and had alibis,' Muckle said. 'The drivers were on the buses.'

Vern snapped her fingers and they all looked at her. 'Look what just happened. That young tech clapped Sparky and she didn't even notice Muckle. Now I know this is a different environment, but hear me out. What if there was somebody out there who was waiting for the kids? We said that Alice might have been targeted rather than just snatched, so what's one thing that would've made her come to him?'

'A dog,' Muckle said.

'Correct. What if it wasn't only somebody she knew, but he lured her away with a dog? It happens all the time with perverts trying to lure kids away. She would have seen him, maybe come over to speak to him and clap his dog. It was somebody she trusted. Somebody she knew. He could have told her that he would drive her home, that she wouldn't be in trouble. Maybe it was a puppy, and she got to hold him or walk him while he held the umbrella. A golf umbrella strategi-cally placed would have hidden his face.'

'Christ, I think you've got something there,' Stewart said. 'Barclay, get in touch with Dunbar and tell him what we think. Get the parents to make a list of people their daughter would have trusted.'

'I'll get right on it, sir.'

'Right. Good. Let's get out of here before that fucking wee window-licking bastard annoys me again.'

ELEVEN

It was late afternoon by the time they were finished. Harry called the team and told them they would meet at ten the next morning.

'Nobody wants to work at the weekend, but we need to get cracking on this,' Harry told Dunbar.

'Aye, that's fine, Harry. I'll have a conference call with Tom Barclay, see if we have anything. You having a drink tonight?'

'I'd love to, mate, but I promised Alex I'd take her out for a meal. Maybe I could persuade her to come over to the hotel bar later. I'm assuming you're staying at the usual place, round the corner from me?'

'We are indeed. Robbie even broke his piggybank so he could buy us a drink.'

'As much as I'd like to, I'm celibate now.'

'Away and don't talk pish. That means you've

stopped shagging. Well, I suppose that does fit, but it doesn't mean you can't put your hand in your pocket, and I don't mean for you to play pocket billiards again.'

'What do you mean, *again?*'

Harry laughed as he drove them back down to the hotel. He knew this was a hell of a job sometimes; you had to laugh or else the thought of young kids being murdered would throw you over the edge.

'I'll let you know about having a wee scoop later, pal,' he said as Dunbar and Evans got out of the car.

'We'll be there, Harry. We'll get a bite to eat first. Catch you later, pal.'

Harry drove round the corner to his flat at Comely Bank, hoping that Chance being there had put Alex in a better mood. Her hormones had been summoning the firing squad recently, and no matter what Harry did, there was always something to criticise. When he had told her he was going to pick up Lillian, her face could have shattered a mirror.

In the flat, he could hear Chance talking, and the sound of his son's voice made him smile. He opened the living room door and saw Chance standing at the window near the small dining table there, talking on the phone. He turned round when he saw his father enter the room and cut the call.

'Hello, Chance. How you doing, son?' Harry

wanted to ask who was on the phone, but he didn't want to sound like his old man.

'Great, Dad. That was Katie on the phone. I know we said we could get a pint, but would you mind if it was during the week? I haven't seen her in a wee while and –'

Harry held up a hand. 'It's fine, son. I was young and in love once.'

'Notice how he says *once*,' Alex said, waddling into the room holding two cups of coffee.

'I meant I was and still am,' Harry said, feeling his cheeks burn.

Chance took one of the cups and sat at the table.

'How's Katie doing?' Harry asked, eager to change the subject of whether he did or did not still love his wife. He felt there was no real answer here. If he said he didn't, then he would be the biggest bastard who'd ever walked the earth. If he said he did, she would accuse him of lying. So it was best to start talking about something else. That usually worked.

'She's doing fine now. Her mum passing suddenly hit her hard,' Chance said. 'She got left the house in her mum's will.'

'That was a shame. But is Katie still enjoying being a police officer?'

'Are you kidding? She wants to be chief constable. She loves it.'

'That's good,' Alex said. 'She'll go far. Just like you will.'

'Eh, listen, if it's all the same to you, would you mind if I spent a couple of nights at Katie's house? She managed to get the week off too. I know I said I would stay here all week...'

'It's fine, son,' Harry said.

'He was young and in love once, remember? He knows what it's like,' Alex added.

'Thanks. Both of you,' said Chance. 'I'm going to shower, then get changed. We're going to go out for a meal, and then, well, you know. Go back to her place for a movie.'

'Go. Enjoy yourself,' Harry said. *And for fuck's sake, don't get her pregnant.*

'Cheers. But just give me a shout if you need me for anything.'

'Where are we going for dinner?' Harry asked Alex as Chance left the room, taking his coffee with him.

'I'm not bothered. Really. I was sick this afternoon and I have little appetite. Why don't you see what your team members are doing?'

'I don't go out with them on a Saturday night.'

'Just a Saturday morning.'

'Jesus, Alex, are you still going on about me picking up Lillian?'

'Of course not. I'm not jealous. What's there to be

jealous about? I mean, I'm fat and ugly, and Lillian is young and gorgeous.'

'She's not gorgeous. She's one of the team.'

'Aye, well, give her my love when you see her next.'

'Alex, come on now, that's not fair. We work together. We're colleagues.'

'*We're* colleagues. We started off as friends. Look at us now; you've knocked me up.'

'You're my wife. It's my job to knock you up.'

Alex got up from the couch, tears running down her face. 'Do what you like, Harry,' she said, leaving the room.

'Oh, come on, love...' he started to say, but it fell on deaf ears.

He would leave her alone for a little while. Give her a chance to cool off. It would all be over in a couple of months and she would return to normal. Harry loved his wife and no woman had caught his eye since he had been with her, and he knew this was a rough patch due to something she couldn't control. He would be patient with her, give her the time and space she needed, because at the end of the day, he didn't know what he would do without her.

TWELVE

Harry wished that Alex had changed her mind and come out for a bite to eat. He had offered to bring in a chippie, but she had then suggested that he go and have sexual intercourse with his own person.

He couldn't remember Moira, his first wife, being like this when she was pregnant. Granted, she had been a few years younger than Alex was now, but there wasn't that big a gap.

He had thought about taking a chippie in for her anyway, but the last time he had done that, she'd been going full tilt with her head down the pan. Of course that had been his fault too.

He had an idea as he stood outside his stairs. The sun was going to be hanging around for a wee while longer, although it was already in its pyjamas, getting ready for bed as it started to pop down in the west.

He took his phone out and called Jimmy Dunbar. 'Hey, Jimmy. Have you eaten yet?'

'*Naw. Fatso's almost eaten his wardrobe he's that hungry, but we're waiting on Vern and Muckle coming through from Glasgow. We're going to grab a bite somewhere, but a place where we won't be leaving Sparky for too long. Why? Where are you? Ready for a wee sesh already?*'

'Not exactly. Alex is having a wee huff to herself.'

'*I'm not surprised. Her hormones will be all over the place.*'

'Can I join you lot when you go to eat?'

'*Christ, of course you can, pal. Me and Heid-the-Baw are waiting in the hotel lobby. Pop round. Muckle will be here in about ten minutes. The way he drives, Vern will have chewed through the fucking seatbelt by the time they get here.*'

'Magic. I'll be round in a few.' Harry hung up and walked away from the tenement building. He turned the corner and headed down to the main road. The hotel was just across the road, outside the Edinburgh Academicals sports ground.

Dunbar was waiting at the hotel's front door for him. As Harry approached, a black Ford Galaxy pulled up. The driver of the car honked the horn and rolled down the passenger window.

'Harry!' Muckle McInsh shouted.

Vern was in the passenger seat and Harry could hear Sparky in the back. The back passenger window rolled down, and Harry wondered if this was a trick Muckle had taught his dog, but then Wee Shug's face appeared.

'Muckle! Shug! And Miss Vern,' Harry said as Dunbar walked down the path to the pavement.

'It's just Vern now. Those two have lost all respect for me, Harry.'

Dunbar looked in at Vern. 'I have to admit, Vern, that you're walking a tightrope going out with that reprobate.'

'What reprobate?' Robbie Evans said, coming up behind Dunbar. 'Some other reprobate you know?'

Dunbar looked at him. 'No, I meant you.'

'Don't worry, Vern, I still respect you,' Evans said.

'Jesus. You'll be telling us you wash behind your ears next.' Dunbar shook his head. 'Anyway, anybody got an idea where we can get some scran? Bearing in mind we have the dug in the back. Harry?'

'Anybody in the mood for a chippie? I know somewhere we could go and eat it.'

'Aye, magic!' Muckle said, and they all agreed this would be a good idea.

Harry took his phone out and dialled a number.

'There's just one thing...' said Muckle.

'Don't tell me you've turned vegan or something?' Dunbar said.

'No, it's not that. It's the car pulling in behind me.'

Dunbar looked at it, then back at Muckle. 'Tell me I'm dreaming, son.'

'Sorry, Jimmy, but he insisted on coming through.'

Dunbar watched as Calvin Stewart extricated himself from his car and came round onto the pavement. 'Even the fucking fresh air smells posh through here,' he said. 'Is this the gaff where we're staying?'

'I don't know if they have any spare rooms, sir,' Dunbar said.

'Fuck that for a game of soldiers. I'll give them no fucking spare rooms. You pair of shaggers can share a room and one of you can give me yours.'

'Erm, I'm not sure that would work, sir,' Evans said.

'How no', son?'

'It's just...you know...'

'Naw, I don't fucking know. Or do you mean *you* want to share a room with me?'

'It's fine, you can have my room. I'll share with DCI Dunbar.'

'Will you fuck,' Dunbar said.

Harry looked at them. 'I think I have the solution.' Then, to his son on the phone, he said, 'Chance? Remember you said if I needed anything...?'

THIRTEEN

With their chippies in hand, they drove the short distance to Katie's house, just off Queensferry Road.

'Thank you for helping us out, Katie,' said Harry, who was the first one into the kitchen.

'That's fine, sir. The house is lonely these days.'

'I'm DSup Calvin Stewart from Helen Street station in Govan,' the big detective said, barging into the kitchen. 'And it's duly noted that you stepped up to the plate when called upon. You, young lady, are going far. Trust me on that. Same with Harry's son. You two are spectacular officers. Now, where's the lav? I'm dying for a pish.'

'It's the door opposite the living room, sir.'

'Cheers, hen.'

'Larger than life, that man,' Dunbar said as Stewart went in search of the toilet.

'You sure you're okay with Muckle, Shug and Vern staying here with Sparky?' Harry asked Katie.

'Of course. It's fine, sir.'

'Terrific. I really appreciate it. They found a room for DSup Stewart in the hotel. Don't worry, we'll make sure you get a stipend for this. You won't be out of pocket. And you have the added bonus of my son staying over.'

Katie blushed.

'Here, away with yourself,' Dunbar said. 'You're making the lassie blush. I'm sure young Chance is sleeping on the couch.'

'Aye, he is that, sir.'

'Told you. Manky sod. Never mind him, Katie. Mind like a bloody sewer.'

'If your face gets any redder, planes will be landing outside on Queensferry Road,' Harry said, smiling at her.

They all took their chippies through to the dining room, except Katie and Chance, who sat at the little table in the kitchen. Sparky thought it was his birthday as he sniffed everybody in the hope of getting some chips.

'His food's out in the car, so don't go spoiling him,' Muckle warned everybody. 'He'll con you with his wide eyes.'

Calvin Stewart laughed. 'Did you see that wee

fanny O'Toole's face when I shouted at him earlier? Jesus, he tried to let me have it the first time I met him.'

'That was a big mistake,' Evans said.

'It was. I gave him such a fucking roasting.' Stewart poked a meaty finger at Evans. 'You know me, son, I treat everybody the same. Give them the benefit of the doubt and then we go from there.'

Dunbar swallowed some fish. 'No, you don't. You told me that you think everybody you meet is an arse-hole. If they turn out differently, then that's a bonus. If they do turn out to be an arsehole, then you say, I told you so.'

Stewart looked at him for a moment, then laughed. 'Aye, you're right. Except that lassie through there. She saved our bacon, so she goes right to the top of the good guy list.'

They chatted about things in general until all the chip wrappers were done, and Stewart gave Sparky some chips for 'shouting at that wee basket-weaving bastard' in the leisure centre.

They chatted for a while, Vern talking about her dog and umbrella theory.

'That's a good call,' said Stewart. 'That wee lassie knew her abductor. We'll try and narrow it down. She lived in Edinburgh, so whoever took her came from here. It wouldn't be somebody from Glasgow. All of those bus drivers had an alibi, and the teachers, so it had to be somebody else. Someone who knew that the kids were going to be there. He had to make sure wee Alice would be there and he came prepared. She was definitely targeted.'

Harry told him that Alice's dad was a mechanic for the same company that had been chartered to drive the kids to Glasgow that day, and that he still worked there.

'Have another wee look at him. Harry, have one of your team do a background on him. Finances, the works.'

'Will do.'

'Then we'll meet up at your station tomorrow. That's handy, it being along the road from the hotel,' Stewart said.

'It is,' Dunbar said.

'Try and keep young Evans there away from the bar. We all need to be with it tomorrow.' Stewart stood up from the table. 'Right. I'm away. I need to get to my kip.'

He said goodnight to everybody and left, and the rest of them tidied their wrappers away.

'Anybody coming down for a nightcap?' Dunbar asked.

'I'm going to get my stuff in and feed the boy here, then I'm going to FaceTime the missus and see how our

Beagle's doing,' Muckle said. 'Catch you at the station tomorrow.'

Harry gave him directions.

Evans said he would stay and chat with Vern for a while, and Katie and Chance were going to watch some Netflix. Shug was going to call his husband.

'You sure we're not putting you out, hen?' Muckle asked.

'Absolutely not,' said Katie. 'It's good to have some life in the house again.'

'You'll be getting a stipend for this, but we'll have a whip-round as well.'

'Just you and me for a swifty then, Harry?' Dunbar said.

'Lead the way.' Harry looked at Chance. 'Behave yourself, mind.'

'Dad, come on now. I'm a big laddie.'

Harry smiled at his son, feeling his heart about to burst with pride. He'd gone from wee boy to man overnight, it seemed.

'Vern, if Robbie tries to take advantage of you, just give me the word and I'll have a wee word with him,' Dunbar said.

Vern laughed.

'Remember and put your Wee Willie Winkie jammies on before you put your lights out,' Evans said to Dunbar.

'I'll put your fucking lights out in a minute.'

That was their version of 'see you later', and Dunbar left with Harry.

FOURTEEN

Harry parked in front of his flat and looked up to see the living room light on. Should he call Alex? He could either tell her he loved her or stir up a hornet's nest. It could go either way.

'Poor lassie,' Dunbar said. 'If she's anything like my Cathy, she won't know if she's coming or going. Her head will be all over the place. I nearly had to wear a fucking tin helmet when Cathy was pregnant, but we got through it. You will too.'

'Aye, I know, Jimmy.' Harry looked up again before locking the car, and they walked through the cold evening darkness to the hotel.

'Young Robbie's got a thing for Vern then?' Harry said.

'Aye, he has that. And thank God. After he went out with that old boot before Christmas, I thought he was never going to find somebody. But he and Vern like each other apparently. She'll be good for him if they stick it out.'

They went into the hotel bar and Harry stopped dead for a second. 'Oh, shite.'

'What is it?'

'Over there. Sitting at a table on her own.'

'Who?' Dunbar started looking around.

'Easy. Don't look, for God's sake.'

'You shouldn't have been all dramatic, making me look in the first place.' Dunbar looked at Harry and shook his head. 'Who am I not looking for?'

'That lassie with the red hair, sitting at a table on her own. Looking down at something.'

'It's not one of your exes, is it?'

'No, it's DS Lillian O'Shea, who you met earlier today in the incident room. If Alex knew we were in here at the same time, well, let's just say the chance of me having a second child with her would be nil, because I'd never be allowed to touch her again.'

And just at that moment, Lillian O'Shea looked up and smiled and gave a little wave, then went back to what she was doing.

'Christ, now what?' Harry said.

'God, you're like a wee laddie at the school dance who doesn't know whether he's going to get his end away or not. Let's go and say hello.'

'Crap.'

They walked over to the table.

'Hello, Lillian,' Harry said.

'Oh, hello, sir. Hello, DCI Dunbar. What are you both doing in here?'

'I'm staying here while we work this case,' Dunbar said. 'We just popped in for a nightcap. What about you?'

'This is my local.'

'Saturday night and you're in a hotel bar with a bunch of old men instead of out on the town with your pals?'

'It's a long story. I just come in here for a quiet drink now and again.'

'Get you a refill?' Dunbar asked, pointing to her near-empty glass.

'I don't want to spoil your evening,' she said, 'but thanks anyway.'

'You're not spoiling anything,' Harry said, 'but if you want to be left alone, we won't intrude.'

She smiled and then looked at Dunbar. 'If you're sure. Bacardi and Coke, please.'

'Coming right up. Harry, you sit down and I'll get them in. Usual?'

'Aye, thanks.'

Harry sat down opposite Lillian and felt a twang of guilt hit him. If Alex walked in now, it would be like history repeating itself, when his former girlfriend had thought he was cheating on her. God rest her soul.

'You come in here often?' Harry asked. *Jesus*. 'Sorry. I just meant I haven't seen you in here before.'

She laughed. 'I used to drink along in The Bailie, but...well, as I said, it's a long story. I drink here now. I started coming here a few weeks ago.'

'This isn't my local, but I come here now and again when Jimmy comes over. I usually drink along the road at The Tap, or in Diamonds.'

'There we go, ladies and gentlemen,' Dunbar said, putting two glasses down on the table before going back for his own.

He sat down with a lager and they clinked glasses.

'We had dinner along at a friend's house,' Dunbar said, 'and we were chewin' the fat over the case. A colleague said that she thought wee Alice was lured away by a man with a dug, and since it was pouring down that day, he could also have had an umbrella, which would have made it easy to shield his face.'

'I was thinking the same,' Lillian said. 'We'd talked about Alice knowing her abductor, and that dog theory makes sense. If he was through in Glasgow, then he had to know the area, and if it was somebody Alice knew, he had to have been told where they were going and at what time. That's what I think. He isn't working alone. I'm not saying that there were two of them there waiting, although that is a possibility, but somebody might have tipped him off.'

'Good thinking,' Harry said.

Dunbar looked at him. 'Alice's dad is a mechanic for Walter Scott Travel. His boss, Mike Morton, is friends with Sandra Robertson's dad. And Morton's wife is a teacher at the school where Alice went and she was there on the day Alice was taken.'

'Was this Morton woman Alice's teacher?' Lillian said, her Irish accent becoming more pronounced.

'No. She was there with her own class,' Dunbar said.

'The investigators went through them at the time. Frank Miller and his team. Agnes Morton wasn't a suspect,' Harry said.

'Now we have the wee yin back, we're thinking about this investigation in a new light,' said Dunbar. 'For instance, we know that he didn't take her and kill her, like it was thought at the time. He kept her alive for five years. And if her cause of death was carbon monoxide poisoning, then maybe it was an accidental death. It could be that Alice's death and Sandra Robertson's were unintentional.'

'And he had to get rid of them,' said Lillian, 'but he couldn't drive around with dead bodies on display in his car, so he wrapped them and put them back where he'd found them.'

'There's a possibility that wee Zoe Harris is still alive,' Harry said. 'If it's the same guy who took her, of course. Just because she went missing on the same day, that doesn't connect them for sure. But if he did snatch her from Burntisland and she was with the other two girls and she *is* dead, then there's a good chance he'll put her back there.'

'I wonder why he felt the need to dump them back at the same place instead of, say, burying them in the woods,' said Lillian.

'I hope one day we get the chance to ask him. I'm hoping Zoe is still alive,' Dunbar said.

'We can only hope, Jimmy.' Harry drank more of his lager and then got another round in.

They had a couple more, then Dunbar said he had to go and talk to his wife on FaceTime, which meant he was going to say goodnight to his dog, Scooby.

'See you in the morning,' he said, leaving the two of them behind.

'I'm going to get home as well,' Harry said.

'I'll walk across the road with you,' Lillian said, finishing her drink off.

They went out into the chilly night. A bus pulled away from the stop and whizzed past. Taxis were heading back into town to pick up more fares.

'You like living down here?' Harry asked as they crossed the road.

'I do. It's a great area.'

'I know you're filling in for Alex just now, but if the position became permanent, would you take it? I mean, we could do with an extra sergeant.'

'I'd love to, but I'm not setting the bar too high. I went into this knowing it was only to cover maternity leave, but I thought I would get a lot of experience from it.'

They entered Dean Park Street, then walked round to the right, heading along to Lillian's street.

'Is it a man?' Harry asked. 'If it's not too personal a question.'

'I don't follow.'

'That made you change pubs. Are you avoiding a man? I mean, it's none of my business; I just know what it's like. Alex had the same problem.'

'Oh no, nothing like that. I've never been married and I left a long-term relationship behind a long time ago. I just had a falling-out with a friend of mine. I don't want to bump into her.'

'What about your other friends?'

'They're mostly in the force. You know what it's like; a lot of your friends don't want to be your friend anymore when you join up.'

'I know. Try being in Professional Standards, investigating other cops. They avoid you like a leper after that. Luckily, the team I lead aren't like that. They're a good bunch.'

'I know. I asked about you before I accepted the position, and if I hadn't felt comfortable coming to work for you, I would have given it a miss.'

'I'm glad I meet with your approval.'

Lillian stopped. 'Well, this is me.'

'Right. Sorry about us having to go in on a Sunday, but there are two teenage girls missing and I'd like to liaise with the people who are looking for them.'

'No need for apologies, sir. It's our line of work. Criminals don't take weekends off. There's a good chance they're connected.'

'Could be, but he took younger kids the last time, if it is the same guy. Unfortunately, there are a lot of them going around.'

'Aye, I know. We need to catch this scumbag soon.'

'We'll do our best, Lillian.'

Harry shrugged into his coat for a second as a cold wind hit them.

'Well, goodnight, sir,' Lillian said.

'Goodnight. See you in the morning.'

Harry waited until she was up at the door to her stairs, then she gave a small wave as she went in and he walked away, round the corner to his own flat.

Upstairs, Alex was asleep in bed. Harry slept on the couch.

FIFTEEN

'These tattie scones are belters,' DSup Calvin Stewart said as Jimmy Dunbar came into the dining room of the hotel. 'I've just asked the lassie for more. Cutting back on the beans, though. I can feel them ten-pin bowling in my guts and it wouldn't do to fart in the dining room. That used to piss off my wife, me letting rip at the table.'

And yet you still don't understand why she left you, Dunbar thought. 'No, it wouldn't do to honk out the room right enough.'

Stewart clacked his knife and fork around his plate, looking up to see where his extra tattie scones had got to. 'I hope that fucking lassie hurries up. I've still got half the scran on the plate and I want to mix it with the scones.'

Dunbar was always amazed at how Stewart could

put his food away and yet didn't look like he had any fat on him. He was a big man, with big hands and a thick neck, and he looked like he could beat a tank into submission, but he wasn't fat.

'Sit down, Jimmy; you're making yourself look like a poorly dressed waiter. But having said that, go and get us both a coffee from the jugs on the table. I'm almost done with this one.'

Please and thank you, ignorant bastard. Dunbar waited for Stewart to slurp the rest of his coffee down and wipe his face before accepting the empty mug.

'Just milk. I'm watching my figure.'

'That's a bit of an oxymoron, sir,' Dunbar said, nodding to the heaped plate. *Emphasis on the fucking moron.*

'Keeping the blood sugar under control is the key, Jimmy. I don't want to end up a fat bastard like you.' Stewart grinned. Dunbar didn't have an ounce of fat on him.

He was tempted to gob in Stewart's coffee, but took it back unmolested and sat down at the table.

'What's that place along from the hotel?' Stewart asked, beaming when he saw the waitress coming with the tattie scones.

'It's a fitness centre. Maybe you could pop along after downing all this. Work it off.'

'Thanks, love,' he said as the waitress scooped the

food onto his plate. 'My colleague here would like some of the same.'

She smiled at Dunbar, raising her eyebrows.

'Aye, go on then. Thanks, hen.'

'No bother,' the young woman said, walking away.

'The only thing I'll be working off is a bottle of Scotch tonight.'

'I can't argue with that.'

'Is that wee bawbag coming down for breakfast?' Stewart said, piling food onto his fork and stuffing it into his mouth.

Dunbar had forgotten all about Evans staying out late with Vern.

'I don't know if he'll have breakfast or not. You know what the young crowd are like.'

'If he's been up the road messing about with that lassie and he's late, he'll hear about it from me.'

'I'm sure he'll be down on time.' *Or the wee bastard will hear about it from me.*

'You spoke to that Morton bloke who owns the bus company. You think he's dodgy?' Stewart asked between mouthfuls.

'I'm not sure he's dodgy, but this is like a jigsaw puzzle that's been emptied out onto a table. The pieces are all there and you can see the picture, but it's not quite there yet. That's the feeling I get from him: he's part of the puzzle, but I'm not sure how he fits in yet.'

'Go and pay him a visit at work. People are more on their guard when they're in their own environment. If the garage isn't open today, we'll jump all over him tomorrow.'

'He was at the Robertsons' house, but aye, I know what you mean. Maybe Harry and I could go along and have a sniff around. I'll get the team to get the exact details of where they're located and we can drop in on him.'

Dunbar looked at his watch and wondered where Evans was. He couldn't blame the laddie for wanting to spend time with Vern, after all the boilers he'd been out with, but he would have felt more relaxed if Stewart hadn't been here.

'I spoke to DSup Percy Purcell before I came through yesterday,' Stewart said, forking more black pudding into his mouth. Dunbar nearly gagged and averted his eyes as the young waitress returned with his breakfast.

'There you are, sir,' she said.

'Thank you.'

'You sure you're wanting your tattie scones?' Stewart asked.

'I am actually. Those few beers last night have given me the hunger.' *So keep your filthy fucking mitts off them.*

'Suit yourself. But what was I saying?'

'Percy Purcell.'

'Oh, aye. Good lad he is. I've met him a few times. He's got a dug like McInsh. But he said he's fine with me being here, since we had one of the victims in Glasgow. I've to keep him in the loop.'

'That was good of him,' Dunbar said, tucking into his own food.

'My arse. What was he going to say? If he'd told me to stay away, I'd have told him to bog off. I was coming through here whether he was having a pissy fit over it or not. But professional courtesy and all that. Besides, if we nab this bastard, he'll be the one who gets to stand in front of the cameras and strut his nob like he's the big cheese. It's a win-win for him.'

'Unless we don't catch this bastard.'

Stewart chewed and pointed with his fork. 'That's not the fucking attitude. I expect more from you, Jimmy.'

An old woman a couple of tables over tutted to her husband and looked at Stewart.

'What got her fucking bloomers in a twist?' he asked Dunbar.

'I'm not a betting man, but maybe she took offence at your choice of vocabulary.'

'Fuddy-fucking-duddy. Anyway, we're going to show the Edinburgh lot that we're just as good as they are.'

'I don't think they look at it as a competition, sir.'

'Pish. You think they would wait until we got home before cracking open the champagne? Don't be so naïve, son.'

'I just know Harry McNeil, that's all.'

'Money changes everybody when somebody pops their clogs in a family. Same with us detectives and collaring some psycho fuck.'

'Can you not use such foul language?' the old woman said.

Stewart had a mouthful of food, but Dunbar was still able to translate that Stewart was suggesting she was an overly curious bovine who was getting on in years.

Just then, Robbie Evans walked into the dining room. Dunbar had never been so glad to see the younger detective.

'Morning, Robbie. You getting some breakfast?'

'I've already eaten. I've been up for ages.'

'Oh, aye?'

'I just thought I'd get up early for a change.'

Stewart laughed. 'Do you think we're daft?'

For a moment, Dunbar actually thought Evans was going to answer that question. 'Grab a coffee and sit down while we finish ours,' he said in a tone that wasn't meant to be argued with.

'Nae bother.' Evans walked away and got a coffee from the thermal jug, then joined them.

Stewart polished off the last remnants of his breakfast and burped. 'I was just saying to Jimmy here that we should check out that wanker who owns the bus company, the one who supplied the bus that took wee Alice through to our city. I want to know everything there is to know about him.' He then let out a belch that would have stripped wallpaper. 'Better out than in.'

Fuck me, Dunbar thought.

'Oh, dear,' the old woman said.

'Jesus, I almost brought that back up. Fucking beans play havoc with me. Lucky it didn't come out the other end or else I'd be flushing my skids down my room's lavvy pan.'

The old woman tutted again and told her husband she thought she was going to be sick. Dunbar wafted a hand in front of his face and pushed his plate away. Evans hid his face in his mug, breathing in the smell of the coffee to stop him chucking up his own breakfast.

'You not having those tattie scones?' Stewart asked.

'Knock yourself out.' *Dirty bastard.*

Dunbar hoped Harry was having a better breakfast.

SIXTEEN

'Look, I'm sorry I was such a bitch yesterday,' Alex said, coming up behind her husband as he sat at the table eating toast and drinking coffee.

'It's fine, honey. I know the wee yin in there is causing a storm and it's not the real you.'

She pulled away from him and sat down opposite. 'You got up early. I didn't even hear you coming to bed.'

'I was quiet,' he replied, which wasn't exactly a lie. He *had* been quiet when he took a cover from the hall closet and draped it over himself on the couch. He was glad Chance was staying along the road.

Alex looked at him for a moment and then something clicked in her head. 'You're working today, aren't you?'

He drank some coffee and looked at her. There was

no getting out of this. 'I have to. Two little girls were dumped, and two teenage girls are still out there, missing. There's no way of knowing if there's a connection yet.'

'God, Harry, I thought we could get out for a walk or something. Even across to Inverleith Pond. Just to spend some time together.'

'You know as well as I do that you'd be with me at work if you weren't...you know...' He waved his next piece of toast in the direction of her belly.

'Knocked up? You make me sound like some wee hoor you picked up.'

'You know what I mean. If you weren't on maternity leave, you would be with me front and centre. However, this is an important case. We're all going in.'

'Including Lillian?'

Harry hesitated. 'Yes. And Eve Ross. And Karen Shiels. All the women I work with.'

She smiled at him. 'I know, I know. I'm sorry I got all...jumpy.'

'Listen, we can go for a walk before dinner. I'll get Muckle to bring Sparky round. Chance and Katie are watching him today, as Vern, Muckle and Wee Shug will be giving us their input. Only Muckle worked the missing girl case five years ago, but many hands make light work and all that.'

He looked across the table at her and knew he was

more in love with her than he had ever been. All the moods, the shouting, the swearing, it wasn't the real Alex. It was the baby inside her that was causing the change, but hopefully when she had given birth, things would go back to normal.

'You know I love you, don't you?' he said to her.

'I know. I hate feeling like this.'

'More sick than you were at T in the Park?'

'That was a breeze compared to this.'

'Plus you could drop your drawers and have a pish anywhere you liked and nobody batted an eye.'

'Get a grip of yourself,' she said, laughing. 'But you're not far wrong.'

He looked at his watch. 'I'd better get a move on.'

'You're the boss. You're allowed to be late. Come back to bed and show me how much you love me.'

'Later, honey, I promise. But if you need me for anything – apart from sex, that is – give me a call. Or even better, call Chance. He and Katie won't be far.'

'Okay, go. Before I throw myself at you.'

He laughed and got up from the table. 'Save your energy for later.'

SEVENTEEN

'Are you trying to fucking kill me, ya hoor?' Dougie Wilson said, stopping for a moment and putting a hand on his side.

'What's wrong with you? Big fanny,' Alec Redfern said, stopping to jog on the spot.

'I think I'm going to be sick.'

'Christ, we're in the street. You going to stand there and let loose like some manky old jakie? Have a word with your fucking self.'

'A wee jog along the beach, you said. Get a bit fresh air into our lungs, you said. What you did not say, and correct me if I'm wrong, was that I would be needing an oxygen tank for the rest of my life.'

'Bloody drama queen.'

They had just run across the Burntisland Links, and now they were continuing across the little bridge that straddled the Fife railway line. Redfern jogged on the spot, looking over the wall. Arthur's Seat sat in the distance, across the cold water.

'We want to be fit, don't we?' Redfern said, his breath blowing out like smoke in the cold morning air. Sunday, first thing, was the best time to go running, with nobody out. 'You ready yet?'

'I'm dying here, Alec. I wish I'd never started this nonsense. I could have been lying in my bed right now, tucked up under the covers. Instead, here I am, running. And not running for my life or anything, just...running.'

'You *are* running for your life.'

Wilson straightened up, hoping this was all going to be worth it in the end. 'Joggers drop dead of a heart attack, I hope you know that.'

'Come on, let's get going. It's downhill to the prom-enade, then five minutes and we'll be back at the car.'

Wilson groaned. He was a lot heavier than Redfern, carrying weight round his belly. Unlike his friend, who was almost stick thin.

They started jogging again, Wilson still lagging behind. Over on the left was the Beacon Leisure Centre, the coloured enclosed tubes of the water slides coming out of one part of the building and going back in lower down.

Wilson thought about how good it would be to just

float on a lilo in the water right now, rather than trying to become a lung donor.

'I told you, didn't I? I told you we'd do it.'

Wilson couldn't take a deep enough breath to tell his friend to go fuck himself, so he kept quiet, concentrating on not dropping down dead.

They crossed the car park entrance at the mini roundabout, the centre on their left now.

'I'm really going to be sick,' Wilson said.

'Aw, what? You're not serious.'

'I am, Alex. I shouldn't have had those bacon rolls before I came out.'

'Bacon rolls? Fat bastard. I told you not to eat anything. Aw, for God's sake. Look at you. You're like a pig that knows it's going to be a packet of bacon at any minute. Jesus fuck. You look like a bag of shite.'

Wilson stopped next to a brick enclosure where the rubbish bins from the leisure centre were kept and heaved against the wall.

'God al-fucking-mighty, that's stinking. Jesus, you're giving me the fucking boak now.' Redfern stepped away from his friend and looked up the elevated concrete walkway that led to the delivery entrance of the centre. He stood stock still, not quite believing his eyes.

A girl was sitting propped up against the brick

wall. She was wrapped in shrink wrap, with only her head and feet showing.

Their jog for the day was over.

EIGHTEEN

There was a murmur in the incident room as Harry walked in. He'd called Dunbar a few minutes earlier and been told they were on their way. *'Me and Robbie and that manky bastard will be there shortly,'* were Dunbar's exact words. Harry didn't want to know.

'Morning, folks,' he said, and at that minute their Glaswegian colleagues came in.

'Anybody got a kettle on?' Stewart said by way of a greeting.

'It's just gone off,' DC Simon Gregg said. At six foot six, he was bigger than Stewart, but not by much.

'Coffee's not going to pour itself, son. Milk, no sugar. And if you gob in it, I'll rip your balls off and give them to Twinkle Toes for a pair of earrings.'

The others looked at each other, wondering which one of them was Twinkle Toes, and Harry wondered if

Stewart had been the victim of a gobbing campaign at one time.

'People, this is DSup Calvin Stewart from Govan, Jimmy Dunbar's boss,' Harry said. 'He's here working the case with us because of little Alice Brent being found in Glasgow yesterday. She'll be brought through here after her post-mortem, which is being carried out today.'

The door opened once more and Muckle, Vern and Shug walked in.

'Where were you this morning?' Dunbar whispered to Evans.

'I told you, I got up early and –'

'Don't talk pish. You never get up early. Did you spend the night at Katie's house?'

'No. I was there late, but we went back to the hotel. I had to get up early to sneak Vern out.'

'I knew it. You had your manky paws all over her.'

'I think I'm in love, boss.'

Vern smiled over at Evans.

'You're like a fucking half-shut knife.'

'Trust me, I've never felt so awake.'

'Aye, well, at least she's around your age, no' got one foot in the grave. What will all the old dearies at your maw's bingo think? No more taking them to the pictures or the dancing. No more eating dinner with them at three o'clock in the afternoon.'

'You're hilarious. I'm sure they'd like to meet you.'

'Hey, I'm a happily married man. They're too old for me anyway. Just right for you, but too old for me.'

'Right, we're all here,' said Stewart. 'DCI McNeil is in charge of this case, but us lot from the west are here to give you input regarding our investigation into the disappearance of little Alice Brent. It went cold quickly, and now we know he'd kept her alive until it was time to dispose of her. We're thinking that her death and Sandra's were accidental, but now our line of thinking is this: is Zoe Harris alive, or did she suffer the same fate?'

One of the phones rang and Lillian picked it up. She spoke to somebody on the other end as Stewart kept talking, then she hung up.

'Sorry to interrupt, sir,' she said to Stewart, 'but a DI Matt Keen from Fife just called. Zoe Harris has just been found. Same condition as the others. Wrapped up. Near the beach in Burntisland, outside a leisure centre.'

'Aw, shite,' Stewart said as the others all looked on, feeling deflated as any hope of finding the girl alive dissipated.

Harry walked up to the whiteboard and looked at the photos of the three girls when they were taken five years ago. He felt his heart sink. Photos of the two teenage girls who had gone missing a couple of weeks previously were stuck on another whiteboard, along with details about them. Ashley Kirby and Simone Santana. He turned to face the others.

'I requested details of the missing girls from CID, because I wanted to make a comparison between them and the girls we now have back. There are a few differences here, but there's one thing that jumps out at me.'

'What's that, Harry?' Stewart said.

'Their ages. Sandra Robertson was twelve when she got taken. She's now seventeen. Alice Brent was ten when she got taken. She's now fifteen. These two girls who were abducted are seventeen and fifteen. Is it just a coincidence?'

'I'm not sure what you're getting at,' Stewart said.

'I know this is a long shot, but hear me out. Whoever took those three little girls wanted to keep them. He kept them for five years, but then something tragic happened and they died of carbon monoxide poisoning. So what if he wants to replace these girls with the ones who just died? The timeline fits. The girls have been dead for a few weeks. What if he realised he wanted two different girls and went out and abducted Ashley and Simone? They went missing three days apart. They've been gone for two weeks now, and suddenly his previous girls are being dumped.'

Stewart nodded. 'That's one theory, especially if

he's a sick bastard. Could be. We won't dismiss it, but we can also work other angles, if anybody has an opinion.'

'They might not be connected at all,' Dunbar said. 'Three different pervs. That's another angle we have to look at.'

'Agreed,' Harry said. He looked at Lillian. 'Can you find out if Walter Scott Travel is open on a Sunday?'

'I'll get on it.'

'If so, tell Mike Morton, the owner, that we'd like to speak to him again. And get a list of all his drivers and run a background check on him.'

'Got it.'

'The post-mortem on Sandra Robertson is being done today down at the mortuary. Ronnie and Eve, I'd like you to be in attendance. You can go now. They'll be expecting you.'

Vallance and Eve Bell nodded and left the incident room.

'DCI Dunbar and DS Evans can come with me to Burntisland. I want to see the scene for myself. Muckle, can you keep in touch with Jimmy's DI, Tom Barclay, and see if he's going to Alice Brent's post-mortem. I'd like to compare notes on both girls.'

'No problem.'

'I'd like to come to Burntisland as well,' Stewart

said and it didn't sound like a request. He turned round to his detectives. 'Which of you is going to have the pleasure of driving me around?'

'I can take my Cortina, sir,' Evans ventured.

'Cortina? What the fuck is that?'

'It's an old classic Ford –'

'I know what the fuck it is. I was saying out loud what everybody else in the room was thinking. We'll take my car and you can drive. If you break it, you bought it.'

NINETEEN

Stewart sat in the front passenger seat. 'So you won't fuck up my radio stations,' he told Evans.

'Trust me, sir, I don't think we have the same taste in music.'

'Why? What do you like? All that loud squealing shite that you jump around to when you're reeking and nobody can tell if you're dancing or needing a pish?'

'Not exactly. I like a bit of country.'

'Country?' Stewart said, spluttering out the word. 'Songs about a guy driving off in his truck with his dug because some fanny has kicked him to the kerb? You're even dafter than you look. What say you, Jimmy?'

'I have to agree with the boss on this one, Robbie. That's a poor show, you admitting you like country.'

'Nothing wrong with a bit of Johnny Cash,' Evans

answered, putting his foot down as they flew over the Queensferry Crossing Bridge.

'I don't know what the speed limit is on your planet,' Stewart said, 'but if I feel like my arse is about to eat the seat, it's time to cool your fucking jets.'

Evans eased off the gas.

'Did you think you were driving your pickup truck down the road, Daisy Duke waving to you in your rearview? Or were you having a fucking stroke?' Stewart said.

'I'm just trying to get us there quickly, sir.'

'Hooring up behind a fucking caravan is only going to get us into the back of a fucking hearse quickly, ya daft bastard.' Stewart turned to look at Dunbar. 'You can drive us back. Evans has forgotten what conveniences a modern car has, like working brakes and indicators.'

Dunbar grinned as Evans looked at him in the rearview mirror.

'A Cortina has all the functioning features of a Fred Flintstone car. What about you, Harry? What you got?' Stewart said.

'I drive an Audi.'

'Nice cars. They go like stink. Just looking at the gas pedal would part your hair. You like it?'

'Nice machine.' Harry didn't add that it was his wife's car.

'Aye, well, Willy Wonka here would do well to get himself a decent motor.'

Evans looked in the mirror as Stewart turned away to look out the window. *Willy Wonka?*

Dunbar just shrugged his shoulders. They both knew Stewart wasn't playing with a full deck.

'Full of chocolate, in case you couldn't put two and two together,' Stewart said, like he had eyes in the back of his head.

Evans had driven up this motorway before and knew to take the A921, heading east for Burntisland. Stewart sat and pointed things out as they drove by, like the Asda at Dalgety Bay, as if he'd never seen a supermarket before. He claimed he would never set foot inside another one since his ex-wife shopped there.

They stayed on that road and took it right down to the Links, and followed the signs for the centre, although the heavy police presence would have guided them if they were about to take a wrong turn.

DI Matt Keen walked across when he saw the car approaching. 'Good to see you again, sir,' he said to Dunbar. They had worked on another case together before.

'Likewise.' Dunbar introduced his boss, and Stewart gripped Keen's hand like he was trying to pop it, but Keen kept eye contact and waited for Stewart to let go.

They had parked in the little gravel car park next to the centre and Keen walked them round to the crime scene. The sun was out and there was very little wind, making for a pleasant day. It would have been even more pleasant if a killer hadn't dumped a body there.

'Two joggers found her earlier. The vomit at the scene is from one of them. He said he was only sick because he'd been running, not because he saw the dead body.'

'Fat bastard, is he?' Stewart asked.

'Not particularly.'

'I used to go jogging, but what a waste of time that was.'

'I can see that,' Keen said under his breath.

'What?'

'I said, you can see here. Where the body was found.'

There was a forensics tent at the scene and a tarp had been draped over the railing on the entrance walkway.

'She was dumped here sometime during the night,' Keen said. 'The leisure centre closed at six and nobody saw anything as they were leaving. The staff, I mean, after closing time. You passed the pub on the other side of the railway line, and that closes at eleven. But even if somebody did see a car go across, they probably wouldn't have wondered why it was there.'

'Especially if they were half-jaked,' Stewart said.

They stepped inside the tent, where the girl was still sitting up against the wall. Her face had the same pink markings as the others. Only her face and feet were showing.

'Good morning, gentlemen. I'm Dr Sarah Coulter, pathologist. I don't believe we've met before.' The young woman smiled at them as they introduced themselves.

'This is a sad ending for this young girl. I cut open the wrapping, as you can see, and there's a dress in there which is too small. DI Keen said that the body that was found yesterday had a dress tucked inside too. Maybe this is the clothing she was wearing when she went missing.'

Harry nodded. 'It is. We have photos of her wearing it tacked up on a board in our station.'

'I'm assuming this place has CCTV?' Stewart said. He looked over at Keen.

'It does, sir, yes. I have one of my sergeants viewing footage now.'

'It's obvious that he didn't carry her here,' Dunbar said. 'He wouldn't have wanted to get caught, so it's most likely he just parked at the pavement and heaved her out.'

'I wonder if he knew the closing times?' Stewart said.

'You can find out anything on the internet, sir,' Evans said.

Harry looked at Zoe Harris. Taken when she was eight, now thirteen. A little girl with her life ahead of her, until some bastard decided to alter the course of history.

'I wonder why he just didn't dump her somewhere less obvious?' Keen said.

'He did this with his other two victims,' Dunbar said. 'One in Edinburgh, one in Glasgow, and now this girl. He put them back where he took them from.'

'Aye, who knows how those sick fucks think,' Stewart said. He looked at the doctor. 'How about a time of death?'

'A few weeks ago. But she wasn't decomposing for all that time.'

'There're signs of her being frozen?' Dunbar said.

'Yes. He kept her somewhere before he decided to dump her.'

'Did forensics find ID on her?' Dunbar asked Keen.

'No. But there was a jotter in there full of drawings. With a name in it; Zoe Harris.'

'I'd like to see it,' Harry said.

'I'll go and get it now,' Keen said. He left the forensics tent.

'Do you all have a family?' Dr Coulter said.

All of the detectives said they had, except for Evans, who didn't think having a mother counted.

'I do too. A son and daughter. Please get the bastard who did this.'

'We're going to do everything in our power,' Stewart said. 'Whatever it takes.'

Keen came back with a clear evidence bag that contained the jotter. Harry pulled on a pair of nitrile gloves and carefully took the book out. It was a typical school book, lined, with a cardboard cover. He gently opened it and saw crayon drawings, starting to get a little better through the pages, as if Zoe had started it after she got abducted and kept drawing in it as she got older.

'Here, look at this,' Harry said to Dunbar and Stewart. He showed them a page with the drawing of a family and a caption: *My family*. Two sisters in dresses with yellow hair, the dad with black hair and the mum with red hair.

'Can you take photos of each page, Jimmy?' Harry asked, passing the book over. He then took his phone out and called Frank Miller. 'I know this is a long shot, but can you remember what colour Zoe Harris's mother's hair was?'

'If I remember correctly, it was blonde.'

'Thanks, Frank. We're at the Zoe Harris crime scene just now. See you back at the station?'

'I'll be there.'

Dunbar put the book back in the bag and handed it to Keen, who left with it to give it back to forensics.

'Zoe's mother had blonde hair, according to Frank Miller. The woman in that drawing has red hair. Even if Mrs Harris has dyed her hair red, Zoe wouldn't know that, and if she was drawing her own family, why wouldn't she have drawn the mother with blonde hair?'

'Which means it's a man and a woman who had her, and the woman has red hair,' Stewart said. 'Right, let's get back to Edinburgh. I want somebody to go and talk to the Harris family.'

'Agreed.'

'And I meant what I said about you driving us back, Jimmy. No offence, son,' he said to Evans, 'but my dug can drive better than you.'

'You should have brought him then,' Evans said under his breath.

'What?'

'I said that's fine, sir.'

'If I had brought him over, he'd have been switched on and bitten you right up the fucking arse. I might be daft, Sergeant, but as I told that wee caber-tossing bastard yesterday, I'm no' fucking deef.'

At least Evans had the decency to pull a beamer as they left the forensics tent.

'I'll keep in touch, Matt,' Harry said.

'I'll make sure you get a copy of the forensics and post-mortem reports, sir. And I'll let you know what we find on the CCTV.'

'Good lad.'

They walked back to Stewart's car, the DSup promising Dunbar a few pints in the bar that night if he didn't 'put us under a fucking bus'. Dunbar always thought it was a good day when he didn't have to be cut out of a car by the fire brigade and accepted the challenge.

TWENTY

Marine Drive was a big rectangular loop with a grassy area separating the two halves of the road down by Silverknowes Promenade.

Abi Peterson squirmed in her seat as she looked out the back window of her dad's car. 'I can see it! I can see it!' she said at the top of her voice. She pointed across to the grassy area down by the promenade itself. 'The bouncy castle!'

Technically, this area was called Edinburgh Beach, and their annual Silverknowes Fair was in full swing. Vendors lined the promenade; there were stalls for the kids to have fun and some small fairground attractions.

'I said we should have tried parking in the Cramond car park further along. The trouble with people is, they don't want to walk the length of themselves,' Colin Peterson said to his wife.

'Och, who wants to walk along the promenade from Cramond when we can park closer?' Nickie Peterson said. 'Look, there's a car coming out.'

'Thank Christ,' Peterson said, putting his foot down in case anybody else grabbed the space, which was unlikely since this was a one-way street. Nevertheless, he raced towards it, put his hazards on and slammed the car into reverse; God help any filthy bastard who tried to nip into the space. There was nobody else approaching and he got the small Nissan into the space without any drama.

'There. Told you. Just listen to me from now on. I'll keep you right.'

Nickie turned to look at her daughter and made a face, causing the eight year old to laugh out loud.

'Aye, double-trouble when you two get together, eh?' Peterson opened his door without looking and a van whizzed by, almost taking the door off.

'Did you see that cock-bag?' he said, standing there and staring as the van rounded the bend at the end of the road and went back along the lower half in the opposite direction on Marine Drive.

'Colin! Not in front of Abi, for God's sake.'

'She doesn't pay attention to what I say,' he said, dismissing his wife. He hoped some of the other parents from the PTA would show up like they'd said they would. He could get together with some of the dads, maybe have a stroll along the promenade to Cramond, where they could have a couple of beers in the hotel, and then Nickie-*fucking-Lauda*, as he called his wife, could drive home. Her driving always improved when he was pished, and he thought she was the best driver in the world when he was lying down on the back seat trying not to toss his bag.

'There's Laura!' Abi shouted, standing on the grass verge on the passenger side of the car. She waved at her friend, who was getting out of a car further down on the other side of the road.

Laura waved back as her mum and dad got out of the car. Her mum opened the rear passenger door and gently took the baby out.

'Can we get a new baby, Mum?' Laura asked.

'We'll see, honey.'

They crossed over the road, Abi staying close by but never taking her eyes off her friend. They started chatting animatedly as soon as they met up.

'Can we go on the bouncy castle?' Abi asked. 'Please, Mum?' She looked pleadingly at Nickie.

'Okay. We'll be waiting outside.' Nickie gave Abi some money for her and her friend and watched the two little girls run off.

Colin started chatting with Laura's father and they

were soon having a laugh, while Nickie chatted with Laura's mother as she carried her baby in the car seat. It was a perfect day.

TWENTY-ONE

When Harry and the team arrived back at the station, they headed to the incident room. Dunbar hung back a little to speak to Evans.

'If you hadn't had such a fucking lead foot, you could have driven us back,' he told the younger detective.

'It didn't seem fast to me.'

'That's 'cause you play those stupid video games all the time. Next time, ease up if he's in the car with us. He did nothing but nitpick at my driving. I'm not doing it next time or else I'll shove him in the boot.'

'If it's any consolation, I got a headache listening to him drone on about how you drive like an old woman,' Evans said, grinning.

'Your heid won't be the only thing aching in a minute.'

'Is it just me, or is anybody else hungry?' Stewart said.

'It's just you,' Dunbar said. 'How in God's name can you think about eating already when you had that breakfast?'

'The secret to keeping the weight off is eating small meals throughout the day.'

Stewart walked into the incident room ahead of Harry, and as he followed Dunbar said to Evans in a low voice, 'He's got fucking worms.'

DI Ronnie Vallance was away at the mortuary with Eve Bell, and Harry caught the others up regarding the body of Zoe Harris.

'I called Walter Scott Travel,' Lillian said. 'They're open today. They have a little service route that goes through Clermiston and to the Gyle Shopping Centre, and they run shuttle buses for the Scottish National Bank's HQ at Gogarburn, dropping people off at several locations, like the Edinburgh Gateway train and tram station, and the Wester Hailes Centre, where they can connect with buses. They pick them up at those locations too, of course.'

'Thanks, Lillian.'

Stewart stood by the whiteboard looking at the photo of Zoe. 'Bastard,' he said. 'She's the same age as my granddaughter. I thought we would get her back.' He turned to the room. 'Pull out all the stops to find this bastard. I don't care if we have to cross the line. We'll deal with that later.'

'I'll have a drive out to Walter Scott Travel now, with DCI Dunbar.' Harry looked at Karen Shiels. 'Can you go and deliver the death message to Mr and Mrs Harris? Take Simon Gregg with you.'

The big detective constable stood up straight. He knew what was expected of them, but it was always hard telling the parents of a dead child that their little one wasn't coming home.

'Yes, sir,' Karen replied.

'Lillian, coordinate things here. If anything comes up, call me.'

'Will do, sir.'

'I need some painkillers,' Stewart said. 'All this thinking about ripping some bastard's bawbag off is doin' mah fuckin' heid in.'

'I don't know if we have any here, sir,' Lillian said.

Stewart pulled a bubble pack from his pocket. 'Like a boy scout, I always come prepared.'

'I know how Stewart feels,' Dunbar said as Harry took the car along Queensferry Road.

'I'm assuming he means it when he said we might have to cross the line?'

'Are you asking as a member of the team or a former Professional Standards officer?'

'Christ, Jimmy, I left that life behind. I know how we work sometimes. I'm not averse to booting somebody in the bollocks if the situation requires it.'

'Good to know. We both know how the courts are in this country. Slap on the wrist, but when some poor sod defends himself and kills his attacker, he's suddenly a vigilante. It's a load of shite sometimes, Harry, and this whole justice system needs overhauling. And don't even get me started on light sentences for fucking rapists.'

'I hear you, pal, but right now it's the system we're stuck with, so we have to navigate it to the best of our ability.'

'Aye, well, God help anybody who touches my wee lassie, let me tell you.'

Harry felt the same way about his son, Chance, and his unborn child. He wondered how he would feel if it was a little girl.

He took Maybury Road and cut along Turnhouse Road by Edinburgh Airport. Old RAF housing was on the right as he slowed down, the entrance to the old RAF base now a business park. A dark-green house up ahead on their right was slowly being reclaimed by nature as trees grew where Harry was sure they hadn't grown during the war.

A sign told them to turn left for Walter Scott Travel. They went past an airline catering group's building on the left and Harry saw a couple of buses further up. Beyond that were trucks and vans for an aviation company that serviced vehicles and equipment used for the planes, like luggage conveyor belts and stairs. Men in dark-blue overalls were moving about as they did their jobs.

It was sunny when they got out the car, but a wind was coming off the airport. The runways were close. Harry and Dunbar stood and watched as a British Airways plane came in to land.

'Can you imagine a Spitfire coming in to land there?' a voice said from behind.

They both turned to see Mike Morton walking towards them. The man smiled and held out his hand. 'Chief Inspector McNeil, wasn't it? And Dunbar?'

'Correct,' Harry said, and he and Dunbar shook hands with Morton.

'What can I do for you gentlemen today?'

'We just wanted a word again. Just some follow-up questions,' Harry said as a train went by on the Fife line.

'Of course. Come into the office.'

They walked across the yard, where two buses were sitting out, gleaming wet in the sun. A hose and buckets were sitting at the front of one of the buses beside a long-reach brush. They were parked in front of an industrial garage with six large garage doors and an office area on the right side. Another small garage-type shed was attached at a ninety-degree angle and had three garage doors.

'Maintenance shed,' Morton said as he saw the policemen looking.

'You do your servicing?' Dunbar asked.

'Not personally, but yes, it's all done in-house. I have a couple of guys who look after the older buses we own, but to be honest, I lease the newer ones for the bank shuttles. The leasing company takes care of any problems; that's the agreement.'

There was a newer-looking bus with blacked-out windows sitting outside one of the maintenance doors. It was smaller than a coach but larger than a minibus.

'That's a midi coach,' Morton explained, seeing them looking at it. 'Twenty-nine seater. It's more economical running that when it's for a small party. It's very popular.'

They went into the office, where a middle-aged woman was sitting behind a desk.

'Why don't you go and have an early lunch, Janice?' Morton said.

'Aye, okay,' the woman said, smiling at them as she grabbed her handbag and left the office.

'We have a wee canteen next door with a coffee

machine and a vending machine. If they want any hot food, they have to bring it themselves.'

Employer of the year, Harry thought.

'Grab a seat.'

'We're okay standing,' Dunbar said.

'Suit yourself.' Morton sat behind a desk. 'What can I do for you?'

'You didn't tell us your wife, Agnes, was a teacher and that she was there the day that Alice Brent went missing.'

'She wasn't Alice's teacher,' Morton said defensively.

'We didn't say she was,' Harry said. 'We just wondered why you didn't mention she was at the leisure centre at the same time Alice was there.'

Morton shrugged. 'I just didn't think.'

'You didn't think to tell us when you were the driver of Alice's bus?' Dunbar said.

'Look, I'm sorry, okay? I just didn't think. We were there for Brian yesterday, that's all. Everybody was emotional. I knew he was a basket case and he's not been looking after himself recently. I told him he should have stayed here, but he wanted to go and fill shelves for a living.'

'What do you mean, stay here?' Harry asked.

'As a bus driver. He used to drive for me.'

'How long ago?'

'Until about six months ago. After his wife died. He couldn't do the driving anymore, he said, and he went to fill shelves for a living. He was convinced that Sandra was going to walk through the door at any moment. Poor bastard.'

'He was a driver when his daughter went missing?' Dunbar said.

'He was. He did some of the service work on the little granny run, as we call it. The shopper bus that goes through Clermiston and Corstorphine to the Gyle. It's mostly old women or young mums. But Brian was our man for the private hires. He liked driving the coaches.'

'He ever get in trouble with the law?' Dunbar asked.

'Like what? Fighting in a bar or something?'

'Or something.'

'You mean interfering with wee lassies, that kind of *or something*?'

'Exactly.'

'We're vetted here. If somebody applied to be a driver and he had some kind of record, he wouldn't be given a job. School work requires us to have a police background check done. Brian isn't a perv. His daughter was missing for five years, for God's sake. And now she's dead.'

'It's happened before that a parent's killed their child,' Harry said.

'Are you suggesting that Brian killed Sandra? She died of carbon monoxide poisoning, you said. Brian told me.'

'How many drivers do you employ?' Dunbar asked.

'Twelve. And a couple of part-timers who do the weekend work.'

'I'd like their names.'

'Why?'

'Do we have to spell it out, Mr Morton?' Harry said.

'It's an invasion of privacy. I'm cooperating with you, answering your questions, but there have been a lot of drivers here over the years. Some of them last a week. One bastard stayed for one shift. I even had another driver who quit halfway through his shift. He called me from his house in Dalgety Bay, saying he wasn't coming back. I had to scramble to get somebody to cover his shift.'

'Dalgety Bay?' Dunbar said. 'We really could do with speaking to him.'

'He's a waste of space. If he asks for his job back, tell him from me that he can go whistle.'

'Anybody else stick out?' Dunbar asked.

'I've had a lot of dodgy bastards through these doors, but sometimes the only requirement I had was for them to be able to steer a bus. Nobody with a criminal record, though.'

'We'll get a warrant for those names,' Harry said. 'And while we're at it, we'll have our friends at the Revenue and Customs tear this place apart. If they even suspect you're using your buses for trips across to France to bring in cigarettes, they'll be so far up your arse with a microscope, you won't be able to sit down for a week.'

Morton sat up. 'I do a few a year, but it's not like we bring boatloads of cigarettes in. Just for personal use.'

'They won't take your word for it. In fact' – Harry turned to look at Dunbar for a second – 'they'll be along today. They don't take weekends off. They'll bring an army with them, especially if the phone call comes from a detective chief inspector.'

Harry looked Morton in the eye as he took his phone out. 'You can call my bluff, or you could give us the driver records. Either way, we'll get those records. A judge will sign off within the hour, especially since kids are involved, and we'll be able to watch Customs rip your garage apart while we're waiting.'

'Alright, alright. I'll get Janice to print them off. How long do you want to go back?'

'Five years. No, make it six,' Dunbar said.

Morton got up and left the office, then reappeared

a couple of minutes later. 'I don't believe it; Janice has left. I thought she was going to take her lunch in the canteen today. Her sandwich box is there. Jesus, some women. Can you come back?'

Harry took his phone out. 'I think I have Customs on speed dial,' he said to Dunbar.

'Give them a call then. Time's running out.'

'Okay, I'll see if I can find the employment file,' Morton said.

Just then, another midi coach pulled in and parked near the buses that were getting washed. Marshall Mann jumped out. Harry remembered him from Brian Robertson's house, when he had come round with Morton and his wife.

Mann walked into the office and stopped when he saw the police officers. 'Have you caught him? The man who took Sandra?' he said.

'No, sir,' said Harry, 'we haven't caught him yet.'

Mann sighed. 'God almighty, it's hard to believe there's a killer out there who killed those wee lassies. Who knows who's next?'

'You worked here long, Mr Mann?' Dunbar asked.

'I just work here part-time to help Mike out. As I said to you before, he's my brother-in-law. I was married to his sister. My wife died.'

'You have a full-time job?'

Mann hesitated for a moment before answering. 'I'm a teacher.'

'A teacher? You didn't mention that yesterday.'

'Oh, I'm sorry. I knew you were busy with Brian Robertson.'

'You came round with Mr Morton here yesterday. Were you were at his house with him when he got the call?' Harry said.

'No, I live just along the road. The cottage on the left at the railway bridge. Obviously, I know Brian too, from the time he was a driver here. I wanted to go along.'

'You're a teacher who moonlights as a bus driver?' Dunbar said. 'Money that bad in the teaching profession?'

Mann laughed. 'No, I'm Mike's brother-in-law. I just do this to help out.'

'Do you teach at Sandra Robertson's school?' Harry asked, but he had a feeling he knew the answer already.

'I did, yes. I transferred.'

'Ah, there it is,' Morton said. He looked at the detectives. 'I've found the personnel file. I'll print out the names for you.'

The printer started whirring and buzzing after a few seconds and spat out several sheets of paper. Morton got up and handed them to Harry.

'I'll have these men checked out,' Harry said.

'Do that. As far as I know, all those men, and one woman, didn't have a criminal record. If you find out they did, then it's got nothing to do with me.'

'Which one lives in Dalgety Bay?'

Morton pointed to a name on the sheet. 'Him. Dougal Dixon. Twat. He worked a month and a bit. Didn't even have the decency to finish his shift that day.'

Harry looked at the sheets. The employment start and end dates were next to each name. 'Some of them don't stay long, you said. Why is that?'

Morton shrugged. 'They think they're coming to work for a huge corporation, but we're a small business here. We pay decent money, but I can't give the same benefits as the big company.'

'How long have you worked here, Mr Mann?'

'About six years, give or take. I started off just washing the buses for a couple of years, but Mike persuaded me to get my licence.'

'Aye, there's always a job here for the lad if the teaching thing goes tits up.'

Just then, Harry's phone rang and he answered it. He spoke briefly to the caller before hanging up. 'We have to go. Thanks for this, Mr Morton. We'll be in touch.'

TWENTY-TWO

DI Karen Shiels parked the car outside a playground across from the blocks of modern housing.

'Christ, I hate this part of the job,' she said.

Simon Gregg, squeezed into the passenger seat, was looking across at the playground. 'Aye, me too.' His own child had died a few years before.

They got out into the sunshine, but Edinburgh was a canny beast and would tempt the unwary out without the proper clothing and then blooter them. To prove its point, it made Karen shiver with a chill wind as they crossed the road.

'Nice area,' Gregg remarked.

'It is.'

The address they were looking for was on the main road, overlooking the playground. Karen wondered if

Zoe's parents ever sat and stared out the window, imagining their child playing there.

They had called ahead, and Mrs Harris had assured them that she and her husband would be in all afternoon. There had been an edge of panic in the mother's voice.

Karen buzzed the button next to the Harris name on the intercom and the door clicked open.

First floor, door on the right. Those were the instructions.

Mrs Harris was waiting for them when they got there, and Karen introduced herself and Gregg as they were shown into the living room without any offer of refreshments. Karen was glad. How could you sit and drink tea when you were about to turn a couple's world upside down?

Mr Harris was in the living room, pacing. He stopped and faced the officers as they came in.

'We've been waiting five years for this visit,' he said by way of introduction.

The room was spotless and Karen noted a toy box in one corner, waiting for its owner to return, now a fruitless endeavour. The corner of the room was rounded, made up of windows, giving the room an airy feel.

'Can you both sit down?' Karen said.

'No, I want to stand,' Harris said, like he was wired

with caffeine. Karen couldn't physically make him but was glad to see Mrs Harris sit down.

'Very well. I'm sorry to tell you that a little girl was found in Burntisland earlier today and we –'

'No!' Harris shouted at the top of his voice before Karen could finish. He took a step towards Karen and Gregg stepped in between.

'Mr Harris, I think it's best if you sit down,' Gregg said to him, holding his arms, controlling the situation in case the man decided to take his grief out on the first available person.

Harris sat down next to his wife and tears started flowing down his cheeks. His wife sat staring, like a film paused near the end because somebody was talking.

'We believe it's Zoe,' Karen finished, her voice softer. 'I am so sorry. There will have to be a formal identification, and we'll arrange for a police car to take you through to Dunfermline, where the post-mortem will take place.'

'Why there?' Mrs Harris said. 'Why not here?'

'Jurisdiction. The pathologist there will take good care of your daughter.'

'I just want her to come back home,' Harris said, starting to cry.

His wife held it together better. 'How...did she die?'

'Initial reports suggest carbon monoxide poisoning, but the exact cause will have to be determined officially.'

Harris stopped crying for a moment. 'Wait, carbon monoxide poisoning? How can you tell?'

'There are certain indicators,' Gregg said.

'How long has she been dead?'

'An estimate suggests a few weeks. I can't go into any more speculation, as we have to wait for the pathologist's report.'

'A few weeks?' Mrs Harris said. 'How can that be? She's been gone for five years.'

'We believe her abductor kept her somewhere.'

'Where?'

'That's what we're trying to establish. And I'm going to ask you some questions, so I want you to think hard.'

The parents both nodded.

'I know you went over this at the time with the police, but can you think of anything that was unusual on the day Zoe was taken?'

Mrs Harris looked at her husband, then back at Karen. 'I'm not sure what you mean by "anything unusual".'

'It was a Friday, so I'm assuming she would have gone to school and come home again before you went over to Burntisland?'

'Yes, she was at school as normal. Nothing unusual. Oh, wait!' Mrs Harris snapped her fingers and all eyes were on her. 'She was upset that day.'

'What about?' Karen said, involuntarily taking a step forward.

'Her teacher was off. She got on very well with him. He was a young man, great with the kids. But for some reason, that day they had a substitute teacher, some old crow that Zoe didn't like.'

'What was her teacher's name?'

'Marshall Mann,' Harris answered right away, without any hesitation.

'What line of work are you in, Mr Harris?' Gregg asked.

'I'm a tram driver.'

'How long have you been doing that?'

'About two years now. Before that, I was a bus driver.'

Karen looked at him. 'Who did you work for?'

'Walter Scott Travel.'

'Beside Brian Robertson and Tim Brent. Tim's a mechanic,' Harris said.

'All three of you had a daughter who was abducted. Didn't you think that was strange?'

'Of course we did. They thought we were being targeted by somebody, but there was no other connection. One theory bandied about was that it could have been one of the passengers. Or somebody out to get Mike Morton.' Harris looked at Karen. 'Seems unlikely now, though, doesn't it? If he kept Zoe for five years. If it was somebody out for revenge, he would have killed her right away, wouldn't he?'

'We can't speculate at this time. I'm sorry,' Karen said. *But yes, they probably would have.*

'It says in the file that Zoe was in the Brownies,' Gregg said. 'Was she in any other clubs?'

'No. Just the drama club, but that was run through the school.'

'Who ran the club?'

'Marshall Mann. Zoe loved staying behind after school for the drama club. They were going to put a play on. I can't remember what it was now, but she loved it,' Mrs Harris said.

Karen looked at Gregg. 'I'll have a family liaison officer come over and she can make the arrangements for you to go to the mortuary in Dunfermline. Again, I'm so sorry for your loss.'

They left the flat and Karen got Gregg to make the call, then her own phone rang. 'Christ, not again,' she said.

TWENTY-THREE

Alex googled the name Lillian O'Shea, but nothing came up pertaining to her being a police officer. Maybe there was some way of keeping that away from prying eyes. Like hers.

She just couldn't shake the jealousy off, no matter how hard she tried. Being cooped up in the flat wasn't helping either, so she had decided to take the matter into her own hands and get out in the fresh air. This whole weekend was ruined because of those girls being found, and she felt like she should be there with Harry, working the case.

She had called Chance and asked him if he could meet her in Inverleith Park, which wasn't that far away, but in her condition seemed like a walk to the moon.

It was nippy, but the wall separating the sports ground from this lane kept the cold in check. She had brought a hoody just in case. Not that she would be able to get it zipped up with her big bump in front, but it would keep the cold off her.

Alex had always wanted children, but now that her first one was well on the way, she'd begun to doubt herself. How would she juggle motherhood with being a police officer? She could just leave and let Harry take care of her, but what if these jealous feelings didn't go away and he was working with Lillian O'Shea every day instead of her? She would divorce Harry, as much as she loved him. It was the easier alternative to sitting and thinking about how he was having an affair every day.

She reached the end of the lane, entered the park and walked towards the pond. She could see Chance and Katie with Sparky, Muckle's big German Shepherd. She liked the big Glaswegian and wondered how his wife felt when he had to leave home for work. Did she get jealous? Probably not. She had her Beagle at home to keep her company, and Muckle was so in love with her that Alex doubted very much that he would stray.

Chance waved, and he and Katie started walking over to Alex. Sparky walked alongside, looking for Chance to throw the ball. He threw it in Alex's direction and she shouted on the big dog. He looked around and saw her and bounded over to where she was sitting on a bench.

'Hello again, Alex,' Katie said. 'You're looking well. Not long now, eh?'

'A couple of months. I can't wait. I just want he or she out of there so I can get my life back to normal.'

Sparky barked at Alex to throw the ball, but Chance picked it up and threw it away from the water.

'How are you feeling, Alex?' he asked her.

'Tired.' She managed a weak smile. 'Feeling out of sorts, if I'm being honest.'

Katie sat on the bench next to her and put a hand on hers. 'You want to talk about it?'

Alex shook her head and looked quickly in Chance's direction.

'Chance, would you mind taking the dog over there to play? I'm worried he'll fall in the water,' Katie said.

'I'm sure he can swim,' Chance said, grinning.

Katie made a sideways motion with her head.

'Oh,' Chance said, cottoning on. He took the dog further along to throw the ball.

'Men,' Katie said, laughing.

'You two seem to be hitting it off. Working in different cities not getting to you?' Alex asked.

'No. It's the opposite. I miss him all the time, but I throw myself into my work. And we meet up on our days off. Glasgow's just an hour's drive away. We each take turns.'

Alex looked at her, feeling glad the younger woman was keeping her hand on hers. It made her feel connected to somebody right now.

'I know you're a couple of years older than he is. Does that make a difference?'

'Not at all. I had a couple of boyfriends before Chance, but they were nothing compared to him. I'm in love with him. But we're taking it easy. I know he's young and he might find somebody else –'

'Let me put your mind at ease; he thinks you walk on water. It's past the infatuation stage now. He loves you. It's not unheard of, young people finding love. I think you make a good couple.'

'You didn't get us here to talk about me and Chance, though, did you?'

Alex shook her head and her smile dropped. For a moment, she felt like bursting out crying, but she held it together. 'It sounds stupid when I put it into words, but Harry has a new sergeant who's covering my maternity leave and I'm worried he'll leave me for her. I mean, I look like a balloon, my complexion can compete with the surface of the moon, I'll need to buy clown shoes for my swollen feet and don't even get me started on the noises my insides are making.'

Katie laughed. 'It's all part of having a baby grow

inside you, Alex. Your body is going through changes, *temporary* changes, and you'll be back to normal in no time.'

'You think I'm just being silly?'

'You're just being pregnant, Alex.' She stood up. 'Come on, let's all go back to my place and have a coffee. The car is parked over on the other side of the park if you can manage that.'

'I feel like I've got a spring in my step,' Alex said. 'But maybe I'd better stick to orange juice or something. And thank you for listening.'

'I have to. You're going to be my mother-in-law one day.'

TWENTY-FOUR

Harry and Dunbar could spot the parents right away; they were the ones panicking and shouting at a couple of uniforms. DI Karen Shiels was there, with Simon Gregg.

'She couldn't have just walked off!' the woman shouted. 'Somebody took her!'

The man standing next to her looked like he wanted to add something but couldn't get a word in. 'Somebody took her!' he finally managed to say, parroting his wife.

'Oh, fuck off, you,' she said, rounding on him, as Harry and Dunbar approached.

'Mr and Mrs Peterson?' Harry said.

The woman turned to him and the young uniform looked relieved. As did Lillian.

'Try to keep calm,' Karen Shiels said, but Nickie Peterson was having none of it.

Harry thought this might have been a pleasant Sunday afternoon, and no doubt that was the intention of the fair organisers, had it not been for the missing girl.

'Calm? Fucking calm? My daughter's missing and you want me to stay calm?'

'Mrs Peterson,' Harry said again, indicating for Karen and Lillian to step away.

'What? Who are you?'

'DCI Harry McNeil. DCI Jimmy Dunbar. Can you tell us what happened?'

Nickie, surprised that these high-ranking detectives had showed up, seemed to expel all the air out of herself.

'My little girl has gone. We were all down there on the promenade, looking around the stalls, and Abi wanted a goldfish.' She looked at her husband. 'It would have got on well with him, since they both have the same fucking attention span.'

'I said I was sorry,' Colin Peterson answered.

'Sorry? It was an easy job you had, looking after our daughter, but oh no, you had to walk along the promenade to Cramond to have a few beers and no doubt ogle some lassie in a skirt.'

'Och, leave it out. She was fine. There was a bunch

of them. Three of us went along for a couple of jars, that's all. And we did not *ogle* some lassie. Christ, what do you take me for? Some perv?'

'No, just a red-blooded man. Can't take your eyes off some women.' Her face was flushed.

Colin shook his head and turned away from his wife.

'We need to focus here,' Dunbar said, and his voice had an edge. 'All this bickering isn't going to help us find your daughter, and right now we need your help.'

'Fine,' Nickie said, tears running down her face.

Harry saw a divorce on the cards for the two at a later date, accelerated if they didn't get the little girl back.

'How old is she?' he asked.

'Eight.'

The number made Harry feel cold inside. Eight. The same age that Zoe Harris had been when she was snatched.

'And you're sure she wouldn't have gone with her friends somewhere else?'

'Her friends are over there. They were at one of the stalls, and when the two of them turned round, Abi was gone. They looked for her, but they couldn't see anything. It's so crowded that all they saw was a sea of faces.'

Harry stepped away from the Petersons and said to

Gregg, 'Have uniforms search all the cars that are leaving, just in case, but quite a few cars have probably left already.'

'Yes, sir.'

Harry saw DI Frank Miller walking towards him, Calvin Stewart by his side.

'We were just talking to the fat bastard who runs the bouncy castle. Right lippy wee fucker he is too. Miller here is going to run his name through the system, but I say we should take all their names. There might be more than one kiddie fiddler working here.'

'Good idea.' Harry looked at Miller. 'We've found out that a teacher who taught at North Merchiston Primary School, where the girls went, works as a bus driver for the same company that was hired to take Alice's class on the school trip to Glasgow.'

'Was he at the centre the day Alice went missing?' Stewart asked.

'He had a day off that day. The boss, Mike Morton, was driving the coach. It was a smaller company then, so he did a lot of the driving himself.'

Karen Shiels was standing nearby and approached Harry. 'Sorry to interrupt, sir, but we spoke to Zoe Harris's parents, and the father is a tram driver, but he's only been doing that for two years. Before that, he was a bus driver with Walter Scott Travel.'

'We knew that back when we were investigating

the disappearances,' Miller said. 'But the case went cold. There was no motive for the abductions. It wasn't our finest hour.'

'Aye, well, now we have the wee lassies back, and there are three other lassies missing, so we're going to do whatever it takes to get them back,' Stewart said.

'We need to take what information we have about the missing girls and compare it to the three victims. Because now we have a third missing child, just like five years ago,' Harry said.

'I've noticed one thing,' Karen said. 'Little Abi is eight, the same age as Zoe Harris when she was taken. The other two are fifteen and seventeen, the same age as Sandra and Alice when they were *found*.'

They looked at her for a moment, waiting for her to carry on.

'Spit it out then,' Stewart said.

'Maybe whoever took the girls two weeks ago was trying to replace the two older girls who died. But then he reverted back, taking a girl who was the same age as Zoe when she was abducted instead of abducting a thirteen year old.'

'Which means?' Dunbar said.

'Which means, maybe he's going to take three girls the same age as our victims were five years ago, starting with Abi. And that means the two girls he took in the past couple of weeks are surplus to requirements.'

'It looks like the girls died of accidental means,' Stewart said. 'It's possible that he didn't murder them.'

'Sandra, the oldest victim, had old restraint marks on her wrists,' Harry said. 'So he's not averse to hurting them, or at least restraining them.'

Stewart looked at Karen. 'If you were this guy, where would you keep them?'

'Somewhere I was comfortable with, but also a place it wouldn't be easy for the girls to get out. A house I owned is the obvious choice.'

'They could have had Stockholm syndrome,' Dunbar said. 'They were only young when they were taken, so maybe he used some kind of threat against them at first. Then, after a while, they became compliant.'

'That's true. It's happened many times before,' Harry said, taking a few steps towards Nickie Peterson. 'Can I ask you where you live?'

'Polwarth.'

'What school does Abi go to?'

'North Merchiston Primary.'

'Who's her teacher?'

'Mrs Morton.'

'Thank you.' Harry turned back to Dunbar. 'Another pupil from North Merchiston Primary School.'

'I thought you were going to say her teacher is that Marshall Mann joker.'

'I want everything there is to know about him.'

'You think he's involved?' Stewart asked.

'I'm not sure. I mean, he was out with a bus and came back when we were there.'

Dunbar approached Nickie. 'When you and your husband parked up, were there any buses, coaches, anything like that?'

She shook her head. 'No. Just cars and a couple of vans.'

'What were the vans like?'

She shrugged. 'Just white vans. One almost side-swiped us.'

Dunbar looked up to where the cars were parked and didn't see any vans up there now.

Harry's phone rang and he stepped away from the others. He answered Ronnie Vallance's call and spoke to him briefly. Then he joined the group again.

'That was my DI, Vallance, calling from the mortuary. Sandra Robertson was around three months pregnant when she died.'

TWENTY-FIVE

Harry was feeling tired by the time they got back to their station at Fettes. They had left Karen, Simon Gregg and Robbie Evans to head up the coordination down at Silverknowes.

A couple of younger CID officers from their own station were there, helping to man the phones.

Muckle McInsh was there with Vern.

'Another wee lassie taken?' he said to Dunbar. 'This is no coincidence, boss.'

'I know. I have a feeling we're being played here.'

'CID are faxing the files on the missing girls through now,' Frank Miller said.

'How's family life with you, Frank?' Harry asked as Lillian got the kettle on.

Calvin Stewart was complaining he was hungry and could 'eat a fucking deid horse right now', and a

CID sergeant reminded him that a local fast-food restaurant served burgers that tasted just like that.

'Anybody else wanting scran?' Stewart said, taking his wallet out. Nobody did, and he gave the young man some money to go and get a KFC.

'I might faint otherwise,' Stewart said, looking at the others. 'I can man one of the phones if need be,' he said.

Dunbar doubted that the senior officer could answer a call in a professional and courteous manner. He watched as Stewart picked up a ringing phone.

'What's that? Fucking Lord Lucan, ya wank? Get tae fuck and stop wastin' my fuckin' time.' He slammed the phone down and turned to the others. 'See? Piece of pish.'

Miller looked at Harry. 'To answer your question – magic, Harry. Wee Annie is toddling about now and Emma is growing up so fast in front of my eyes. How's Alex doing?'

'Having a hard time of it, to be honest. Her mood swings are somewhere between axe murderer and circus chainsaw juggler. I'm in the middle and either tool causing my demise is fine by her.'

Miller laughed. 'Kim was like that. Alex will be back to normal soon. She's not got too long, has she?'

'No. Couple of months. Eleven weeks or so, something like that.'

'Women are funny, aren't they?'

Lillian looked round from the kettle. 'I hope you meant that in a good way, sir,' she said, her Irish brogue now even more pronounced. Harry had noticed that when her back was up, the accent came out thick and strong.

'Of course I did.'

'You're going to get your coffee gobbed in now,' Harry whispered.

'I not only have eyes in the back of my head, DCI McNeil,' she said, 'but I have perfect hearing.'

Harry cleared his throat. 'Where've those files got to?' he said, and a few seconds later, the fax machine spat them out.

'Right,' he said, picking up the papers. 'Ashley Kirby, aged seventeen, and Simone Santana, aged fifteen.' He looked at Miller. 'That's a strange name for somebody living in Scotland.'

'Her father's from Barbados.'

'Right.' He sat down at a desk and Miller and Dunbar sat as well. Stewart sat at a computer, almost daring the phone to ring. The other CID officer was talking on the phone.

'It says here the two missing girls were last seen at the Gyle Shopping Centre, getting on a bus.'

'Are they on CCTV?' Dunbar asked.

Miller shook his head. 'There are two main

cameras on either end of the horseshoe-shaped façade, each one covering the opposite side, but after the girls leave the main entrance, there are buses everywhere. Double-deckers, blocking the view,' he said. 'I don't know if you've been to the Gyle Centre, sir, but outside the main doors there's a canopy running the length of the façade, so it hides people until they step out from under it. The girls weren't seen after they left the main entrance at the front of the building. We checked with Lothian Buses, but none of the CCTV cameras on the buses that were there at the time had the girls coming on.'

'What about taxis?'

'There's a taxi rank in the middle, but a call to all the cab companies proved fruitless.'

'They could have got in a car with somebody,' Harry said. 'I'm assuming the trams have CCTV?'

'They do,' Miller answered. 'The stop is just up from the main entrance, but again, they didn't hop on a tram. Also, there are CCTV cameras at Morrisons supermarket, and if the girls had walked through the underpass to the Edinburgh Gateway railway station and tram stop, we would have seen them. CCTV was checked at the station, and nothing.'

'They leave the shopping centre and what?' Stewart said. 'Maybe they bumped into somebody they knew. Some young bastard with a car. Maybe he got them into it and suggested they go somewhere for a bit of how's your father. They objected and he killed them.'

'I'm assuming their phone records were checked,' Dunbar said.

'Yes, sir. The last time their phones pinged was at the Gyle Centre. No calls or texts were made or received after they left.'

'That's strange,' Harry said. 'What girl doesn't have her phone attached to her hand?'

'None of them,' Lillian said, bringing the mugs of coffee over. 'Not in my experience anyway.'

'Thanks, Lillian,' Harry said, taking a sip of the coffee.

'The only way I can see those girls giving up their phones is by force,' she added, bringing more mugs across.

'Cheers,' Stewart said, looking across at the table where the kettle sat, in case there were any stray doughnuts lying about. Foosty or not, he would have given one a good skelping.

'These girls leave the centre and then bump into somebody they know, and he manages to get their phones off them. Both of them. And there's no struggle that we're aware of. No reports anyway. How the hell did he do it?' Dunbar said.

'I'm going to have a drive over to Dalgety Bay and

talk to this Dougal Dixon, the bus driver who left abruptly halfway through his shift,' Harry said. 'Lillian? You fancy a wee drive?'

'Yes, sir.'

'Anybody else?'

'Aye, me,' Stewart said, just as the young detective came back in with his KFC. 'Better take a pool car. I have a feeling that a seat is going to get some greasy fingers wiped on it.'

He stood up with his bucket of chicken.

'Right, we'll get off,' Harry said as Lillian grabbed her jacket. Then, in a whisper, he said to Dunbar, 'Well, that backfired. Next time, get your hand up sooner.'

Dunbar grinned. 'See you later.'

TWENTY-SIX

'That's a nice accent you have there, Detective Sergeant. Where do you come from?' Stewart said.

'Comely Bank.'

'Is that in the south or Northern Ireland?'

'No, I mean Comely Bank near Stockbridge.'

'Where's that then? My geography is all over the place.' Stewart was already on his second chicken breast by the time they hit Queensferry Road. 'And just remember before you take the piss again that I'll be writing a report on who contributed well to this case. Harry is already getting an A-plus. You, ya cheeky wee madam, are already on a hiding to nothing.'

'Cork,' Lillian said. 'I thought you meant where do I live here, sir.'

'Do you think all of us weegies have sawdust

between our ears?' he said, looking at her from the back seat.

Harry focused on driving the pool car and didn't make eye contact with either of them.

'No, sir, not at all. Just got my wires crossed for a minute.'

Stewart licked his fingers, which Harry saw as a pointless exercise as the DSup was about to pick up another piece of chicken anyway.

'On a scale of one to ten on my talking-pish-o-meter, I have to say that one is nine and a half. It would have been ten if you hadn't taken a beamer.' Stewart then settled back with another piece of chicken and gnawed away at it.

'Christ, I wish I'd got some coleslaw with this. Maybe a wee biscuit and some fries. You like KFC, Lily?'

Harry looked sideways at Lillian to see how she'd react to Stewart shortening her name, and to her credit she took it on the chin.

'I do. Especially the legs. The biscuits are good. My favourite is the chicken breast, though.'

Stewart swallowed what he had in his mouth. 'You can keep your filthy mitts off this bucket. My doctor says to eat small meals, not share them. This is going to tide me over until dinnertime.'

'Is that when your heart's going to explode?' she asked.

Stewart laughed. 'I'll be burning the calories off later, young lady. I might be big, but I'm not fat.'

Harry had to agree. 'I don't know how you do it, sir. I just look at a doughnut and put on half a stone.'

'I have the metabolism of a furnace,' Stewart said. 'That's what my doc said. As long as I keep exercising, I'll be fine.'

He slurped and chewed all the way across the Queensferry Crossing, the second time that day he and Harry had been on the bridge.

'You from around here, Harry?' Stewart asked as they left the bridge. He looked around for somewhere to put the bucket, now empty apart from the bones, and he found the perfect spot for it. The floor. 'As far as anybody knows, that was there when we got in.'

Lillian took a packet of tissues from her pocket and handed them back to Stewart.

'You just might have earned a gold star on that report I'll be writing,' he told her. 'Percy Purcell will get to hear about this and no mistake. Bright young detective like you will go far, I'm sure.'

He wiped his face and fingers, and filed the tissues in the same place he'd filed the bucket.

'I was born and brought up in Inverness,' Harry replied, and Stewart looked puzzled for a second, as if he'd forgotten he'd asked Harry a question in the first place.

'Not quite like that wee teuchter arsehole. He came from the back of beyond. Although I think he said he did a spell in Inverness. No offence.'

'None taken.'

'I don't think he'll last long in Govan. He'll be out on his arse before long. One thing I do not like at all is some lippy wee bastard. Like that wee tosser at the bouncy castle today. I was about to bounce him. Fucking wee midget.'

They drove along to Dalgety Bay. Lillian had called ahead, and Dougal Dixon had told them he would be nipping out to Asda for some messages but would be back in time for a wee chat, making it sound like it was a social event.

'With any luck, the wee bastard will get some Tunnock's Tea Cakes in since he knows we're coming,' Stewart had said, but he didn't hold out much hope. 'Probably fucking digestives, knowing my luck.'

As luck would have it, coffee was on offer when they got to Dixon's house, but the plate of biscuits Stewart had been expecting never appeared. They sat down on the settee while Lillian took a chair. The furniture was leather, or maybe vinyl, but it didn't creak like vinyl.

'He needs to read a book on fucking etiquette,'

Stewart informed Harry when Dixon went back to the kitchen for the sugar. 'I mean, coffee without biscuits. Are we living in the Dark Ages or something?'

Dixon came back in with a bowl of sugar and an attitude. 'Bloody Mike Morton. Did he start telling you things about me? Making up shite about me?' He sat on a dining chair he'd pulled out from the small table in the corner. Only two chairs, Harry noticed. Maybe one for him, one for the prossie he'd had round, in case she fancied a cup of Earl Grey before moving on to the next customer. There were no signs anywhere that Dixon had a wife, or a husband, or any significant other.

Stewart held up a hand. 'We're just here for a wee chat, son.'

'He didn't say anything derogatory when I talked to him,' Harry confirmed. 'He just wasn't happy that you'd left halfway through your shift.'

Dixon made a face. 'Did he tell you he called me up, giving me a rake of abuse until I told him where to shove his bus?'

'No, that seemed to have been left out of the conversation.'

'Oh aye, he started in on me, and I just gave him it back. Told him the truth about what the other drivers think of him. And I told him I wanted a reference for a new job. He laughed and told me to go fu...' He looked at Lillian. 'Fiddle. So I calmly told him I would call Edinburgh Council and speak to the bloke who deals with the bus contracts and tell him about the perv he has working for him.'

All three detectives perked up at that.

'What perv?' Stewart asked, all thoughts of a tea cake now gone.

'That young guy – what's his name again? Marshall Mann.'

'Why do you say he's a perv?' Lillian asked.

'Well, most of the buses come into the yard by eight o'clock at night. There's only one back-shift bus doing the Ratho to Edinburgh run and it comes in at midnight. Anyway, we have to sweep the bus out and mop the floor. Like Morton couldn't afford to hire a bloody bus cleaner, but no, he's such a tight wad. But anyway, a couple of weeks ago, I'd been running behind and got back to the yard about twenty minutes late. It had got dark by then, and I'd just put the bus into the garage and parked up for the night when I heard the last bus coming in. I knew it was that knob Mann driving it.'

Stewart put a hand up. 'Wait. He's a teacher, I thought?'

'This was on a Saturday. He drives at the week-end.' Dixon paused, looking at Stewart.

'Right, carry on, son,' Stewart said.

'Aye, well, there's a door leading into the office area where we leave our time boards and the like, and there's a door with a window in it. I could see right out into the yard where dafty had stopped his bus. Now, it wasn't full dark and he had his interior lights off inside the bus, but the yard lights were on and I could see inside. He had a lassie there. She was helping him, I assumed, walking up and down the bus as if she was checking for lost property. Then I saw her stop and Mann grabbed hold of her and they started kissing.'

'Did you see who it was?'

'Aye. When he'd stopped putting his hands all over her, he opened the garage door and she got off with him and I could see her clearly. I didn't know her name, but I'd seen her talking to him at the Gyle Centre one day during the week. She had a school uniform on. I don't know what school it was, but she looked to be fifteen or sixteen.'

'How come she was on his bus on a Saturday evening?' Lillian asked. 'I mean, how would she be on the bus at the yard?'

'He would drop his passengers off at the Gyle on his last run and then she would stay on. He'd bring her along to the yard, and they'd do whatever it was they were going to do.'

'Did he see you?' Harry asked.

'No. I waited until he was pulling his bus in and

she was back on it with him, then I slipped out the door. I don't know if he heard me start my car up or not, but he didn't say anything the next night. I mean, how could he? He's not exactly going to say, "Did you see me shagging that lassie last night?", is he?'

'Is that why you quit your job?' Stewart asked.

'What? No, of course not.' Dixon paused. 'It was because of the monster.'

'Monster?' Stewart said, starting to furrow his brow. This was sometimes a precursor to an explosion of expletives if he thought someone was being an arse.

'Aye. The monster who lives in the garage.'

TWENTY-SEVEN

Calvin Stewart thought Dougal Dixon was on meth. Or taking the piss. Either one would earn the man a swift kick in the goolies.

'Explain,' Stewart simply said, in a tone that left no doubt what the repercussions would be if Dixon turned out to be some nutcase.

'The monster. Oh aye, I bet Morton didn't tell you about that, did he?'

The three detectives waited for him to elaborate.

'You might think there's something wrong with me,' Dixon said.

'You think?' Stewart said, eyeing the coffee mug, glad he hadn't touched it. They might all end up in a basement somewhere, tied up and being experimented on by aliens, if this bampot was anything to go by.

Dixon looked off into space for a moment before

suddenly getting to his feet. Stewart stood up, his adrenaline kicking in. Fight or flight, and he wasn't going anywhere.

'Right, that's enough of your shite,' he said. 'You seem to be the only fucking weirdo working at that bus company. I think we need to take you back to Edinburgh and have a wee word.'

Dixon snapped back to the here and now. 'No, no!' he said in a panic. 'Please, sit down and I'll explain. I was trying to get my thoughts together.' Then he looked at Stewart with a puzzled look on his face. 'What do you mean, *weirdo*?'

'Have you ever tried walking with an extendable baton rammed up your fucking jacksie?'

'Hypothetically?'

'Try me.'

'Okay, okay, I know what you're thinking,' Dixon said as he sat back down. 'But I swear to God, this is true. I had to go into the small workshop that's off to one side of the main garage, and it was dark. I flicked the light switch, but nothing came on. I had to use my phone, and while I was shining the wee light about, I shone it on a shelf where the cleaning supplies were kept, and there was this face looking back at me. It was hideous, like something out of a horror film. I nearly shat myself.

'Mind, that wasn't the first time either. Sometimes

when I'd been driving on the back shift, bringing the bus back in at midnight, I thought I saw somebody creeping about that old house near the main gate. Looking out the window. She was wearing a nightie or some kind of gown. I thought it was a ghost or something at first, but that face in the workshop was real. I'm telling you, there's somebody living in that house!'

Dixon was on the verge of babbling.

'Right, take it easy, son,' Stewart said, sitting back down but not taking his eyes off Dixon. 'Where do you think this person is coming from?'

Dixon looked down at his feet for a moment, as if the answer lay in the carpet. 'I don't know. I thought the first time that she was a passenger hanging about or something, but then, in the workshop, she turned round and it was as if she was half human, half monster. Her face was gone.'

'What do you mean, gone?' Lillian asked.

'Gone.' He looked at her as if this should require no further explanation, like somebody might want to know all about electrics when you've told them that in order to turn off a light, you flick the switch.

'It was pitch black in there. There are lights outside the garage of course, but she was in the shadows. Then she turned to me and it seemed like she didn't have half a face.'

'Did you tell anybody?' Harry asked.

Dixon tilted his head back and took a deep breath before looking at him. 'No. I mean, what could I do? Sit down with one of the boys at lunchtime, talk about football and throw something into the conversation like, "Oh aye, and by the way, there's some fucking mutant hanging about in here after dark"? That would have gone down well.'

'What happened after the first time you saw her?' Stewart asked.

'I thought I was seeing things. Maybe my eyes were overtired. I left the engine running because it was chilly outside, and besides, the miserable old bastard who owns the place always wants the buses inside. They can't be locked and he doesn't want anybody creeping about after dark, touching his buses. If only he knew. But there she was, at the side of the shed. I thought I was seeing things at first, but then she moved again. That got a fucking spurt on, let me tell you. I went inside by the Judas gate, opened the garage door and got that bus right inside. There's only inches to spare either side, and when you put the headlights out, the place is in darkness. You have to go back round and press a button to bring the garage door down. Then you have to walk along in the dark to the interior door that leads into the wee office where we leave our stuff. Shiting a brick, I was. I grabbed a broom, just in case.'

'You would have swept the floor with her,' Stewart said, and nobody knew if he was joking or not.

'I saw her again a few nights later. Then, when I'd been there for about a week, I saw her inside the garage.'

'Did she say anything to you?' Harry asked.

'No. She just made a noise and ran away through to the back.'

'Did you follow her?' Lillian said. 'Or is that a silly question?'

'I like your sense of humour, that's for sure,' Dixon replied. 'Follow? Aye, maybe with a hunting rifle. That thing was seriously messed-up, facially. There's something going on there. Something not right.'

'Who do you think it is?' Lillian asked.

'I didn't think to make introductions. I mean, please excuse my lack of social skills, but I wasn't going to hang around and ask her if she fancied going to the pictures one night.'

'I meant, you didn't hear anybody else talk about her?'

'Nope. If they did see her, then they were keeping quiet about it, just like me.'

'You never heard Mike Morton talk about it?'

'All he said is, we should never go in the workshop because of all the chemicals that are stored there. If we wanted cleaning stuff, he would get it for us. He's a dodgy bastard, and make no mistake. He's hiding something there.'

'What line of work are you in now?' Harry asked.

'Hospital porter.'

'Were you working today?'

'I was. I can give you my supervisor's number; he'll confirm it. Six until two. I did this job years ago, and I've seen some sights, but nothing like the woman in the garage.'

Dixon scribbled a number down on a piece of paper, and Lillian took it and contacted his supervisor. In a matter of minutes she'd confirmed Dixon's alibi.

'Right, Mr Dixon, we'll be off. You've been very helpful,' Stewart said, not complaining about the lack of tea cakes. The man might have rubbed them about his baws before wrapping them back up again anyway.

'What do you think?' Stewart said once they were back in the car, firing the empty KFC bucket out of the window. 'Fucking smell was giving me the boak already,' he said. 'I like the stuff, but this scrapper of a car is bogging.'

'Just something Dixon said about being a porter; "I've seen worse," he said. Burn victims. What if his ghost is a burn victim?' Lillian said.

TWENTY-EIGHT

Harry was knackered. He excused himself and went into the corridor.

'*Hello?*' Alex said, answering after the third ring.

'Hello to you too. How are you doing?'

'*I'm fine. I'm at Katie's house with her and Chance. And Sparky of course. Any sign of any of you coming home?*'

'Not right now. Did you see Percy Purcell on the news, giving a statement about the wee girl who's gone missing?'

'*I did. What a shame. I'm glad we're erring on the side of caution and getting the public to look out for her.*'

'Me too. It might not be a snatching. She might have wandered off and, God forbid, somehow ended up in the Forth.'

'*You don't think that, though, do you?*'

'Not at all. I think there were perverts down there, and one of them took her. We've asked the public to hand in any photos they took or let us download them from their phones. See if we can see any known offenders. We have CID going to talk to any of them living in a two-mile radius, then we can widen the net.'

'*I rub my belly, knowing our wee baby is in there, safe and sound, but he or she has to come out one day and then be part of this shitty world where grown men and women take children.*'

'Try not to get yourself upset, Alex. I'll be home as soon as I can, but I can't give you a time.'

'*I know.*'

'See you later. Love you.'

Harry disconnected and walked back into the incident room. 'Where's Stewart?' he asked Dunbar.

'Going to have a chinwag with Percy Purcell. They go way back.'

'Sir!' Eve Bell said, holding up a piece of paper. 'We had a phone call from somebody who lives down in Joppa. They might have seen something relating to the Sandra Robertson case.'

'Like what?' Harry asked.

'Like the killer.'

'Aw, that's fucking magic,' Lenny Smith said to his wife. Cathy was unperturbed.

'I had to. There's a wee lassie missing now.'

'Aye, but callin' the polis? That's like...'

'Like what?'

'I don't know. It doesn't seem right, inviting them into our hoose. Sam will be shitting himself.'

'I've already called them. He's on his way over.'

'Christ, what's he going to think?'

'He's going to think we're helping to track down somebody who killed a lassie. And left her dumped on the beach like she was a piece of flotsam.'

Jetsom, Lenny was about to say, proud that he was one of the best at the quiz night in their local on a Thursday night, and he was about to explain the difference, but he kept his mouth shut. Cathy was the one who always raised her voice when she got a correct answer and the cheating bastards at the next table would overhear and scribble the answer down. Some of them looked like a bunch of brain-dead mutants who wouldn't know their own name if it was stitched into their jacket.

The doorbell rang and Cathy answered it, Lenny almost touching cloth. He hated the polis – the way they sneaked around, trying to pin shite on anybody who looked like a good fit-up. He hoped the social wouldn't take his benefits away for this, although he didn't think they would. But the bastards might look on finding a body as working and penalise him.

'Christ, Maggie just told me the fuckin' polis are on their way,' Sam said, rushing into Lenny's living room. 'Do you think the social called them? I'm no' fit enough to go to prison. I mean, an ugly bastard like you will be alright, but they'll ride me like the prison bike.'

'Cheeky bastard.'

'We didnae kill that lassie, we just found her,' Sam said, but Lenny had his eyes wide and slightly shook his head: *That's not what the polis are coming for, numbnuts.*

'Oh.' Sam looked sheepishly at the two wives as they all stood in the living room.

'I called them,' said Cathy, 'because I got up to go to the lav, then decided I'd make a cup o' tea, and I saw something outside. But do tell us more about you finding the body.'

'Look!' Lenny said, pointing out the living room window. 'There's hundreds o' polis invading the place. Aw shite. Good job, Cathy.' He hoped she wouldn't be entertaining the postman while he was inside.

'Shut your pie hole.'

They stood around as if each of them was trying to come up with some kind of alibi, then the doorbell rang.

Cathy answered it and a flood of suits came in, led by some big bastard.

'Right, which one of you is Lenny Smith?'

TWENTY-NINE

Harry wasn't going to point fingers, but he made it clear that it wasn't good form to find a dead body and then just make an anonymous phone call.

'You might have been able to give us some information,' he said. 'Sometimes people remember little details that can help break a case.'

'Are we under arrest?' Sam asked.

'No, not yet. But if we find out you murdered that lassie and dumped her on the beach, I'll make sure you get a whole life sentence so that the next time you're on the outside, it will be in a box,' Calvin Stewart said.

'Tell us what happened,' Jimmy Dunbar said.

Lenny and Sam told the story, embellishing how they'd gone out for a jog along the beach. Omitting the part where they felt knackered by the time they got to the first lamppost.

'Jog?' Stewart said. 'I'm sure the speed you two go at, it might not be considered a jog. Maybe a stroll, if you're lucky.'

'Anyway,' Lenny said, biting his tongue, 'we saw something lying on the beach. We went down to investigate and it was the lassie wrapped in plastic.'

'Anybody else nearby?'

'Nope. Just us. We walked up to the phone box and called it in.'

'And didn't leave your name,' Harry said. 'Why was that?'

'We didn't want to get involved. I mean, we've all seen the crime shows where some daft bastard goes after a witness and kills them. I don't know about you, son, but I don't fancy being wrapped up like a Marks and Sparks chicken sub and dumped on the beach.'

'What about you?' Dunbar asked, nodding to Sam.

'I'm with him. We did the right thing by calling you, but I don't want to end up in prison, falsely accused of something we didn't do. We did our civic duty. Far as I'm concerned, we didn't break the law.'

'Nobody's accusing you of anything,' Stewart said. 'Yet. So just tell us what you saw. Any suspicious vans or buses parked up?'

'There wasn't anything,' Lenny said. 'Not when we were there.'

Ronnie Vallance came out of the kitchen with Eve Bell. Harry thought it must have been a tight fit, since Vallance was no lightweight.

'Mrs Smith saw a minibus parked down at the bus stop when she looked out of the window yesterday morning, sometime after two o'clock,' he said.

'Any writing on it?' Harry asked.

'She said yes, because the bus was white, but being up this high and with it being dark, she couldn't make it out. It had blacked-out windows too. And it wasn't one of those little ones either. This was a larger, squarer one. Her words.'

Harry stepped closer to Lenny and Sam. 'If you think of anything else, give us a call. You two seem like decent lads. You're not being a grass, but you could end up being a hero if you remember something and it helps us catch this scumbag.'

'Aye, nae bother,' Lenny said.

'We have officers doing a door-to-door. Hopefully, somebody else might have seen something.'

Sensing there was nothing more to be had out of them, the detectives left.

Back at the station, they slumped down on their chairs at the desks.

'I think we should call it a night,' Stewart said. 'Uniforms and CID are still out at Silverknowes. The search is going to be called off shortly because it's dark, but everybody will be there again at first light tomorrow. Agreed, Jimmy?'

Dunbar looked at Harry, who nodded. Agreed.

THIRTY

Calvin Stewart plonked himself down on the most comfortable chair in Katie's living room as the others dished out their Chinese meals onto plates.

'How you feeling, honey?' Harry said.

'No' so bad, sweetheart,' Dunbar answered with a smile.

'Listen, pal, I could do a lot better than you.'

'You already have,' he said, nodding to Alex.

'I hate to interrupt what you two have going on,' Alex said, holding a little plate with some lemon chicken and white rice.

'You're quite safe, Alex,' Robbie Evans said, dishing out some food. 'Glad you could join us.'

'Me too. Thanks for inviting me.' Alex smiled at him, then went to find a seat to take the weight off her feet.

'Sparks, no,' Muckle said to his dog, whose nose was at the same level as the table. The Shepherd wagged his tail and went to sit next to his master.

Harry put a hand on Katie's arm as she was walking past. 'Thanks again for putting up with us,' he said. 'DSup Stewart has made sure that Police Scotland will foot the bill for this lot, and he's already put in for the stipend for putting our guests up. And as I said earlier, we're going to make sure you're taken care of. No arguments.'

'Please don't worry about it, sir. I'm just glad to have you all in the house. It fills it up and makes it less lonely.'

'Just make sure my laddie helps you with the clearing up.'

She laughed. 'I will.'

They were in the dining room, crammed around the table, some sitting, some standing. There was general chatter, then the conversation turned to the case. Lillian was sitting next to Vern and they were chatting away.

'I was talking to Tom Barclay this afternoon,' Muckle said between mouthfuls of rice. 'There were no witnesses to the dumping of the body at the leisure centre, but one young lad said he thought he saw a minibus parked there earlier. He thought about tanning it, but went on his way.'

'Did he say whether there was any writing on the side?' Stewart asked. 'Or get a number?'

'No, nothing like that. He thought the place was maybe opening up again, but there were no other cars or buses there.'

'I'll give Tom a call and get him to canvass the area again. The press officer is getting us on the news tomorrow,' Dunbar said.

Lillian looked over at Stewart. 'Sir, while you were away to Joppa with the team, we were tossing around ideas regarding the two latest missing girls, Ashley and Simone.'

Stewart swallowed his food and washed it down with some water. He didn't want any carbonation to fill him up. 'And what did you come up with?'

'We were thinking about what the girls were doing in their spare time leading up to their abduction. Comparing notes about each girl. They were two years apart in school, so we wondered if they socialised with each other after school. Their friends said yes. However, there was one other thing they had in common.'

There was silence in the room now. 'Come on then, Lily, spit it out. The floor is yours.'

'They rode the same school bus.'

'I thought that was an American thing?' Alex said.

'So did I,' said Lillian. 'But it's a thing here. I'm not

sure about every school, but up at Broomhouse High, there are such a lot of kids getting out at once that they would overwhelm the public transport system. It's because they share the grounds with St. Francis's. Two schools emptying out would be a nightmare, so they put on school buses. They sit on South Gyle Broadway. The kids get on an assigned bus and it goes round a pre-determined route, and they get dropped off at certain points.'

Harry clicked on what she was getting at. 'Are the buses from private contractors?'

'Yes.'

'Ashley and Simone got on one run by Walter Scott Travel?'

'Yes, they did. They sat near the front, so whoever was driving would have heard them talking.'

'It's possible,' Harry said. They had talked about their little trip over to Dalgety Bay. 'We have nothing concrete, though,' he continued. 'A lawyer would have it laughed out of court, and we have no grounds for getting a search warrant. We need concrete evidence that something is going on. So we'll keep on digging. Mike Morton's drivers are hiding something, I'm sure. That bus company is connected somehow.' He went on to tell them what Dougal Dixon had said about the teacher, Marshall Mann.

'I still think that's a bit ropey, him being a bloody

teacher and a bus driver. I mean, they're not the best paid-people, but it just doesn't ring true,' Stewart said, finishing up his fish supper and looking for somewhere to throw the wrapper away. He eyed up a nice spot behind the couch but then handed it to Alex, who had put her hand out for it. 'Cheers, Alex. You'd get a promotion for that if you were based at my station.'

'I'm sure Robbie would like a promotion.' She smiled at Stewart.

'I'm sure he would, but he didn't take my chip wrapper away.' Stewart dug his pinkie nail between two teeth.

'Shove your promotion up your arse,' Evans said in a low voice so only Dunbar heard it.

Stewart looked across at him, and for a moment Evans thought the DSup had heard him. He shovelled a handful of chips into his mouth.

'That halfwit Dougal Dixon also told us that a bus goes to the Gyle Centre on its last run, drops passengers off and goes off-service to their base along the road at the back of the airport,' Stewart said. 'It got me thinking. Ashley and Simone were last seen there, and they couldn't be spotted on CCTV from the centre. We know those Walter Scott buses don't have CCTV like the Lothian ones do. What if those lassies got on the bus and stayed on because they were flirting with the driver? We know Marshall Mann has a thing for young lassies being on his bus. Dixon told us he'd seen Mann with a teenager on his bus along at the garage. What if they got on his bus and he took them along there?'

There were murmurings in the room.

'We'll go along in the morning to talk to Morton and ask him who was driving the midday shift when the girls went missing,' Harry said. 'Also, Lillian, check out the woman who works in the office, Janice something. Her full name is on that list. She skipped off pretty quickly when we were there.'

'Will do, sir.'

'What if this Mike Morton doesn't want to give us the name of the driver who was working that Saturday?' Evans asked.

'We'll let Muckle slip Sparky off his leash,' Dunbar said.

Stewart stood up. 'Right, laddies and lassies, I'm getting down the road. I'm knackered.' He put a hand on Evans's shoulder and leaned in close. 'Like I told that wee windae-licking forensics bastard, I'm no' deef.'

'Aw shite,' Evans said to Dunbar once Stewart was gone.

Dunbar laughed. 'You and your big mouth. Don't worry, Spunky, I'll put in a good word for you.'

Most of them were finishing up, and they agreed

they should all get some rest and meet in the office at nine the next day.

'I think I'll hang around here for a wee while,' Evans said as Vern and Muckle helped clear up.

'Will you fuck,' Dunbar said. 'You think I'm going down to breakfast on my own to listen to Stewart slavering a load of pish? I don't think so. If I have to sit beside the radge at the breakfast table, so can you.'

'Aw, come on, boss,' Evans moaned.

'Come on nothing. You'll have plenty of time to see Vern when you get back home.'

'I'll only be ten minutes.'

'Five minutes if you keep your boots on? Get t' fuck down the road. I mean, I can't physically force you, mind, but see that new lassie, Lillian? She'll be promoted long before you. In fact, she'll be getting a telegram from the Queen congratulating her on her diamond wedding before you get a promotion, and the lassie's no' even seeing anybody just now.'

'The Queen will be deid long before that.'

'Nobody likes a smart arse, Robbie.'

'Look, boss, I promise you I'll be down in that dining room alongside you tomorrow. Just tell me when you want me to chap the door.'

'Seven thirty. Wee bastard. Don't say I'm not good to you. And God help you if you're one minute late.'

'Cheers, boss.'

Dunbar shook his head and smiled at Evans behind his back. 'Young and in love. Who'd have thought it?'

'We were young and in love once,' Harry said. 'Just not with each other. You know what I mean.'

'Aye, say it a wee bit louder, mucker, I don't think the guards at Edinburgh Castle heard you. But talk about young love, here's your bride now. Get home before she hears you babbling.'

THIRTY-ONE

The next morning, their roles were switched: Alex was chipper and Harry felt knackered.

'She seems nice,' Alex said, sipping her hot tea at the dining table.

'Who?' Harry said, fiddling with his tie. He was giving serious consideration to wearing a bow tie from now on. He had never been any good at doing up a tie, making it either like a string or some huge fat thing that barely reached down past his chin.

'Lillian. I was chatting to her last night when we were having dinner.'

'Were you? I didn't see you talking to her.'

'I was. In the kitchen.'

'What, did you warn her off with a carving knife?' He pulled the tie out again and left the living room, going back through to the bathroom mirror.

'Don't be silly. We just chatted, colleague to colleague.'

She sat and looked out the window for a little while.

'What did you say?' Harry asked, coming back into the room.

'I said, Lillian and I just chatted. She seems nice.'

'She *is* nice. She's good to work with. She's a good detective.'

He went back out and finally nailed it with his tie in the bathroom. He felt agitated, having to constantly explain himself to Alex. Hopefully, she would stop going on about Lillian and see she wasn't a threat. Harry was looking forward to becoming a father again and he didn't want the memory soured by Alex's mood swings.

'You want anything for breakfast?' she asked as he came back into the living room.

'No, thanks. I'm going over to the hotel to meet Jimmy in a little while. I don't feel that hungry.'

'I could do you some toast or something.'

He looked at her smiling face and nodded. 'Okay, some toast, then I have to go.'

'Imagine having your seven-months-pregnant wife running after you like this,' she said, laughing.

'I have a different take on it, mind. Nobody's going to believe you.'

'Where's the young lassie from yesterday?' Stewart complained as Dunbar approached the table. 'That fucking old closet who's on today hasn't been through yet and it's gone seven thirty. Fuck's sake.'

The old woman at the next table with her husband started fanning herself with her hand.

'How long you been sitting here, sir?' Dunbar asked, inconspicuously looking at his watch.

'Fucking ten minutes. She must think I'm on hunger strike or something. I'm bastard well starving.' Stewart looked at Dunbar. 'Don't just stand there like a lemon, Jimmy. Get your arse planted.'

Dunbar sat down, took his phone out and sent a text to Evans: *Two minutes or I'm going to boot your fucking bollocks.*

'Morning, sir,' Evans said, coming into the dining room. He heard the ding of an arriving text, took his phone out and looked at it.

'Who's that?' Stewart said, demonstrating no respect for privacy.

'Wrong number. Some fanny sending me nonsense.'

Dunbar stuck his boot out the side of the table, unseen by Stewart, and pointed to it. 'Grab some coffee for me and you, will you, Sergeant?'

'Absolutely.'

Evans walked away as the old waitress came in.

'Give me the works, with extra tattie scones,' Stewart said. 'There's a big tip if you can nash, 'cause we're late for work.'

'Coming right up, sir. And for you?' she asked Dunbar.

'Me and my other colleague are having toast and cereal,' he replied, smiling at her. He knew service workers were overworked and didn't need customers like Stewart hassling them.

'They work hard for their money here,' Dunbar said to Stewart once the waitress had left.

'Keep your fucking Y-fronts on straight there, Jimmy. I was nice to her, wasn't I?'

'Do you think you could watch the language?' the old man said.

'Sorry, boss. I didn't realise you were earwigging.'

'We are not earwigging, to use your parlance, but you have a voice that carries like a foghorn.'

'That's a fucking compliment,' Stewart said to Dunbar.

'Oh dear,' the woman said, tilting her head back as her face turned red.

'Look what you've done, you oaf!' the man said, standing up and fanning his wife with a cloth napkin. 'She's having a flush.'

'You should maybe leave her alone at night then, pal. Gie her a wee rest.'

'Filthy swine.'

Evans came back as the old man got perilously close to the table. 'Sir, we're police officers. Maybe just ease up a bit there. It's not worth it. Pretend you're deaf for half an hour.'

The man looked at Evans. 'Okay. But tell your sergeant there to tone it down.'

'I will.' Evans set two mugs of coffee down. 'The old man there said to tell you to tone it down,' he said to Stewart, smirking. 'Sergeant.'

'Well, since you're the boss, you can run the investigation. Jimmy and I will be going fishing today instead.'

Evans went back for cereal.

'The only fish I like are wrapped in newspapers,' Dunbar said. He got up and chose a little box of cereal, then sat back at the table.

'Right, we should get along to that bus garage early. Then we can talk to that Marshall Mann wanker,' Stewart said.

'Oh dear,' the old woman said.

The waitress came with Stewart's breakfast.

'Magic, sweetheart. Extra tattie scones. You're a star.' He slipped a twenty under the milk jug.

Evans sat down with a box of Rice Krispies.

'You eat like a wee lassie,' Stewart said. 'Hard to believe you're such a fat bastard when you eat stuff like that.'

Evans wasn't quite as skinny as Jimmy Dunbar, but he was nowhere on the road to being fat.

'I'm only big where it counts,' Evans retorted.

'Aye, yer heid.'

Harry walked into the dining room and approached the table.

'Would you like a full Scottish, sir?' the waitress said.

'Oh, I'm not staying here. I'm just here for my colleagues. I can wait outside.'

'Bollocks,' Stewart said. 'You hungry?'

'A bit,' Harry said, feeling his stomach grumble when he saw the food.

Stewart took out another twenty. 'That's for you, sweetheart. Stick the extra breakfast on my bill, if you don't mind.'

The older woman smiled. 'Right away, sir.'

'Grab a coffee, son,' Stewart said as the waitress scuttled away. 'We were talking about that clarty bastard Mann. Having wee lassies on his bus. I'd like to see his background. I know he's a teacher and a bus driver, but surely there's a chink in the armour somewhere?'

'Just because he passed the background checks,

doesn't mean to say he isn't a dirty bastard,' Dunbar said.

A couple of minutes later, the waitress returned with Harry's food.

'Thanks, love,' Stewart said. He pulled the twenties from under the milk jug and handed them to her. 'Take that now. There are a couple of dodgy customers here,' he said, nodding sideways to the old couple.

'Cheers for this,' Harry said. 'Alex burnt my toast.'

'Nae bother, pal. But what do you reckon to this ghost bollocks Dougal Dixon was talking about?'

'He didn't seem to be the sort who would make up weird stories, don't you think?' Harry said.

Stewart poked a fork in the air between bites. 'I've seen them all, Harry, but I think you're right. I don't want us asking this Mike Morton about it, though. Might put him on his guard.' More tattie scones.

They sat and bandied ideas about until Stewart and Harry had finished their breakfast, then Stewart went back up to his room to brush his teeth. Harry took his phone out and turned the camera on, checked there was nothing stuck between his own teeth and popped a Tic Tac.

'Christ, he's larger than life, eh?' Harry said about Stewart.

'He is,' said Dunbar. 'Upstairs would have had him

booted out a long time ago if he wasn't known as Teflon. Untouchable.'

'How come?'

'He took a bullet for two kids. Bank robbery. He stepped in front of them as stray bullets started flying and he took two. Saved the lives of the bairns. He's a hero.'

THIRTY-TWO

The team were already gathered in the incident room. Frank Miller was sitting beside Eve Bell, looking at something on the computer.

'Morning, sir,' Miller said to Stewart.

'How's things?'

'Fine, sir. We've been doing background checks on all of the staff at Walter Scott Travel.'

'Make for interesting reading?'

'Actually, it does.' Miller stood up and addressed Stewart and the others. 'Mike Morton had a complaint against him when he worked as a bus driver, before starting his own company. A woman was drunk and had fallen asleep on the top deck. Morton said he went to shake her by the arms and then she woke up, confused and unsure of where she was. *She* said he had his hand on her boob and was touching her. She started

screaming, and he went and called for backup. When
the police got there, she was outside, puking. She made
a formal complaint, but the fiscal threw it out, saying
there was no evidence, Morton had a clean record and
the woman had also accused a taxi driver of the same
thing.'

'What happened in that case?' Harry asked.

'The taxi driver had cameras inside his taxi and
kept them running when he saw she was drunk in the
back. He didn't leave his seat and called for the police.
When they got there, she accused the cabbie of assault,
but he showed them his camera footage. A report was
sent to the fiscal, but no further action was taken when
she saw the footage. It makes you wonder about
Morton, though. Considering that two girls went
missing.'

'Aye, we're going along to the bus company to have
another word with him. How did the checks come back
for the other drivers?'

'Clean, sir.'

'Including Dougal Dixon?'

'Including him. Clean as a whistle.'

'What about Marshall Mann?' Dunbar asked.

'He's been suspended from school,' Miller said.

'Oh, aye?' Stewart took a step towards the
computer. 'What did he do?'

'There's been a claim that he and a seventeen-year-old girl were meeting up after school. Rumours. There's nothing to substantiate it, but they've put him on administrative leave in the meantime. The girl is denying it, but she was friends with Ashley Kirby, the missing teenager.'

'Wait a minute,' Harry said. 'Ashley and Simone didn't go to Mann's school. He teaches at North Merchiston.'

'*Did*. He transferred to Ashley and Simone's school two months ago. They were needing a teacher, he applied because he specialises in English, and he got the job. He was suspended three weeks ago.'

Harry looked at Miller. 'Let's say he goes there two months ago, and he's been driving the buses part time with Walter Scott for the past, what, five years? He could have known those girls and known they took the school bus. He could have driven them home. Eve, can you check and see if they had him as a teacher?'

'Right away.' Eve Bell got on her computer, looked up the number for the school and called the number.

'If they did,' said Harry, 'then they wouldn't have seen him as a threat. Even if he was suspended, his brother-in-law, Morton, has still been letting him drive. Being suspended from teaching doesn't affect Mann's part-time job.'

Eve hung up and looked at them. 'He was their English teacher.'

'Thank you,' Harry said. 'Let's say he was put on the school run, or asked for it, and he was their driver and they sat and chatted with him. The other kids wouldn't have suspected anything, because maybe the other drivers were chatty. I mean, just being friendly without being pervy. But what if Mann found out the girls were going to the Gyle Centre that Saturday, or even arranged to meet them there? He would have known his upcoming bus schedule, and maybe he saw an opportunity.'

'Let's get along there,' Stewart said. 'Miller, stay here and coordinate things at this end. Lily, come with us.'

They left the station.

THIRTY-THREE

Stewart, Dunbar and Evans took the unmarked car, which still smelled of KFC, and Harry drove Alex's Audi, Lillian in the passenger seat. Two patrol cars followed.

'Your wife has good taste in cars,' she said.

'But not in men, apparently,' Harry replied, following the unmarked car, in which Robbie was doing his best to keep to the speed limit. 'I'm the man who knocked her up, so I'm the cause of all her pain, real and imaginary.'

'Oh, that's not nice, sir. She's pregnant. You men have the easy part.'

'I feel this conversation is going downhill, so I shall attempt to divert it onto something else.'

'*Pet Sematary*. The movie based on the Stephen King book. Original or remake?' Lillian said.

'Original. You?'

'The remake was good and scary, but I remember being scared by the original. It was so creepy.'

'Agreed. Not that I was scared, you understand,' Harry said, not wanting his manhood brought into question.

'Of course not.'

'Alex loves all those scary movies. Me? I prefer a good thriller.'

They chatted about books and TV shows until they were driving along Turnhouse Road towards the business park. They saw a couple of buses on the left as they crossed over the railway bridge that carried them over the Fife line.

The unmarked car slowed down, turned into the business park and stopped for a second, presumably for Dunbar to give Evans directions or to say a prayer for getting them there in one piece.

They stopped the cars in front of the office, next to two single-decker buses. White with the company name on the side. Everyone got out of the vehicles.

'I'm no' saying that my life flashed before my eyes or anything, but I'm sure I had a conversation with my mother and she's been deid for ten years,' Stewart said to Harry, a slight sheen on his forehead.

'Taxi driver just birled right in front of me, but I took evasive action,' Evans said. 'You're welcome.'

'Welcome?' Stewart said. 'You never told us you learned to drive on a fucking tractor. You know, in a field where there are nae other vehicles and the only daft bastard standing near you is a scarecrow.'

'What can I do for you gentlemen today?' Mike Morton said, coming round the front of the bus next to them. 'And lady.'

'We need to have a word, Mr Morton,' Harry said. 'In your office.'

'Okay. No problem.'

Morton led the way in, and just as they were entering, Janice, the secretary, got up from behind her desk and left. Harry turned towards Lillian and nodded.

Lillian walked over to the little red Renault parked round the side by some other cars and stood by the driver's door. A few seconds later, Janice appeared, pulling her coat on.

'Oh, God, you scared me,' she said, jumping back a little.

'Going somewhere, Janice?' Lillian asked.

'Er...just popping out for some milk for the tea.'

'That can wait. Why don't we find somewhere we can sit and have a wee chat?'

Janice's shoulders slumped. 'We have a wee canteen. We can have a cuppa in there.'

'Let's go.' Lillian nodded for one of the uniforms to come with them.

They walked back through the door Janice had come out of and went inside.

She plugged the kettle in and they sat at one of the small tables. The room was adorned with bus timetables, posters for buses and a calendar that had been donated by a motor oil company. Two vending machines stood facing them. Otherwise, it was bare. Lillian could see through the grimy windows across to Edinburgh Airport and she watched a plane coming in to land.

'This is some place,' she said as Janice poured two mugs of coffee. The uniform stood by the door.

'You want milk?' Janice asked Lillian.

'I thought you didn't have any?'

Janice gave a wry smile. 'I lied. There, you caught me out.'

'Milk, no sugar, thanks.'

Janice poured and sat down opposite Lillian. 'Is this about Marshall?'

'Could be. What can you tell us about him?'

Janice hugged her mug for a few seconds and blew on the hot brown liquid before taking a sip, trying to get her thoughts in order. 'I've been seeing him for a while now. I can't help it. I'm forty, divorced, no man in my life. I go home to two cats, who I love dearly, but I have physical needs. Marshall was there to lean on when I got divorced, and things went from there. We're not doing anything wrong, though.'

'Nobody's saying that you are. I just wanted to have a little chat here, rather than asking you to come to the station.'

'That would be embarrassing. And a little exciting. I've never been in a police station before.'

'Trust me, when you're on the receiving end, it's not fun.'

'What is it you want to ask me?' Janice asked.

'First of all, where were you going when we came in?'

'Around to see Marshall. Mike was just getting in with the extra bus that's put on for the rush hour. I tell him that I have to go out and get some supplies, and he lets me go without question. He answers the phone and does some of the admin work in the office, so he doesn't mind me going to get stuff.'

'But you go and see Marshall Mann instead?' Lillian said.

'Yes. He lives round the corner and I go to his house.'

'Isn't he married?'

'Oh no, his wife died.'

'When did this happen?'

'A few years ago. I'm not sure exactly when. He

doesn't talk about her much. He doesn't have any family either. He lives on his own, so we're not disturbed.'

'Is he at home now?'

'Yes. He'll be expecting me.'

Lillian nodded. *He won't be expecting me,* she thought.

'How long have you worked here?'

'A couple of months. It's hard to get a job when you're my age. I was lucky to get this.'

'And the benefits are good too.' Lillian drank some of the coffee.

Janice giggled. 'I suppose so.'

'You know Marshall's a teacher too, don't you?'

'Yes, I know that. He's taking a break at the moment.'

'Is that what he told you?'

'Yes. He needs to get a break from the kids sometimes.'

'He likes the kids, doesn't he? Especially the young girls.'

Janice looked puzzled for a second. 'What do you mean?'

'Did he tell you he was suspended from the school?'

'What? No, he isn't. He's taking a break.'

'He's been suspended on suspicion of seeing one of the pupils from his school. She's seventeen, so she isn't a minor, but it's inappropriate nonetheless.'

'A girl? He wouldn't do that. You know what some of those schoolgirls are like. They think they're the teacher's girlfriend.'

'Did you know he taught the two teenagers who were abducted a couple of weeks ago?'

'No, I didn't know that. Look, this is just a coincidence. He's a good teacher, so it's natural that some girls might have a crush on him.'

'He's the teacher of two missing girls. There's no smoke without fire, Janice.'

'What are you trying to say?'

'Can you think of anything that you might have found...strange? Maybe something that made you feel uneasy?'

'No...nothing,' Janice answered, looking down into her mug.

'Are you sure?' Lillian said, looking across at her and not taking her eyes off her.

'There was just one thing a couple of weeks ago. It bothered me at the time, but I didn't say anything.'

'What was it?'

'I went round to his house on the Sunday. We were going to have lunch. He was off, so he said we could have a fun afternoon. When I went round, he was washing the dishes in the sink. And over to one side, there were three wine glasses. With a little bit of wine in the three of them. As if he'd had two other people round.'

THIRTY-FOUR

'We want to talk to you about Marshall Mann,' Stewart said, turning his nose up. The office was old and he could imagine the ghosts of RAF officers past. The only nod to anything post-1970 was the computers on the desks.

Harry, Dunbar and Evans were behind him, followed by a couple of uniforms.

Mike Morton and his wife, Agnes, were sitting at separate desks.

'What about him?' Morton said, immediately on the defensive.

'Where is he?' Harry asked, looking around.

'He's not due in yet. He's doing a midday shift.'

'Easier to pick up wee lassies that way, I suppose,' Dunbar said. 'I mean, he likes to bring wee lassies back here on his bus when he's finished his shift, doesn't he?'

'What are you talking about?' Morton twisted his face into a look of disgust.

'Have you come here just to hassle us?' Agnes said. 'We can be on the phone with our lawyer in a matter of minutes.'

'You know what we're talking about,' Stewart said to Morton, ignoring Agnes. 'He's your brother-in-law. It makes it easier for you to cover up. Look the other way. Is he married?'

'Marshall? No. He was, but his wife was killed in a car crash a few years back.'

'Now he's after wee lassies because his wife is deid? You might think we're a bunch of brain-deid arse-holes from the west, Morton, but I can assure you we're anything but.'

'I'm not suggesting anything like that, but I haven't seen Marshall with any wee lassies, as you put it.'

'What time are you here till?'

'The office is usually closed by six thirty, seven. The drivers know what to do when they come in. They don't need us here.'

'Did you know that Mann has been suspended from teaching?' Dunbar asked.

'Aye,' said Morton. 'Just because he talks to his pupils like they're human beings, he gets accused of wanting to fucking wench them. God forbid he should treat them like adults.'

'That's because they're kids,' Harry said, suddenly imagining his yet-unborn child in a school uniform being leered at by a teacher.

Agnes chipped in, 'Our bus drivers are friendly to everyone. We get compliments all the time. There's no harm in being nice to the kids.'

'Come on, they're seventeen, some of them. They're switched on nowadays. They're the product of the social media age,' Morton said.

'Simone Santana is fifteen. She's still a minor,' Stewart said. 'Tell us where Marshall Mann lives We want to go and talk with him.'

'He'll be here in a little while. Besides, I'm assuming you checked him out. You'll have his address.'

'He rents his old flat out. That's his address. He's moved but we don't know to where. So tell us.'

'I can't do that, not without a warrant.'

Stewart stepped closer to Morton and both Harry and Dunbar saw the man flinch in his chair a little. 'Listen here, I am going to make one phone call, and not only will we have a fucking warrant, I'll have friends of mine in the press come crawling round here, looking for the alleged paedo who owns this shitey wee bus company. They'll be all over you like a rash. Then I'll call the twat in the council who overseas contracts for wee bawbags like you and tell him you're allowing some paedo teacher to drive schoolkids. You might as well wipe your arse with your operator's licence after that because that will be all it's good for.'

Agnes had a face like thunder. 'Just tell them, Mike. The sooner they're out of our hair bothering us, the better.'

'Jeez, somebody got out of bed the wrong side. Why didn't you just ask?' said Morton, putting a brave face on it. 'He lives just round the corner.'

'Round the corner? Where round the corner?'

'Well, actually *on* the corner. Turnhouse Road and Turnhouse Farm Road. You can't miss it. Turn right out the gate and it's on the left after you go over the railway bridge. It's a wee cottage there.'

Stewart stared Morton in the eyes. 'You call Mann and I'll make sure you're both sharing a cell. If he's done anything, you'll be an accessory. Both of you.'

Morton remained seated behind his desk and the uniform watched over him.

The detectives piled into the pool car, after having a chat with Lillian about how her interview with Janice had gone.

Dunbar was behind the wheel, Evans in the back, shaking his head. Learned to drive on a tractor indeed.

THIRTY-FIVE

The drive took thirty seconds, as there was no traffic coming along the road. Across the Fife rail line, like Morton said, and Turnhouse Farm Road was on the left, and they could see the little cottage from the main road.

Round the corner, Dunbar parked the car in the driveway. A small hatchback was parked further in and now they were blocking it.

The house was a long, single-storey cottage which looked well-kept.

'Bit isolated here,' Stewart said. 'Perfect if you're a beast.'

They walked up to the door facing them and it opened before they got there.

'I'm not a religious man, so you're wasting your time,' said Marshall Mann, pretending not to recognise them at first. 'Oh, it's yourselves, detectives. Come away in. I've got the kettle on.'

They followed him inside. The place smelled fresh and clean with a hint of furniture polish. If he was a hoarder, he hid it well.

'Living room's through here,' Mann said.

All of the detectives were on high alert. If somebody jumped out, Evans would be expected to lead the defence, Harry and Dunbar next, in that order, with Stewart providing backup with a couple of flying boots.

The only sound was a plane coming in, seemingly about to land on the roof.

'You get used to it,' Mann explained.

'How long you lived here, son?' Stewart asked.

'About four years.'

'It's a nice property,' Harry said, looking around. There were photos sitting on a dresser. Mann with a woman, dressed in climbing gear, sitting on bikes, in canoes, walking a trail up some Highland mountain.

He saw Harry looking at the photos. 'That's Denise, my girlfriend.'

'Is she around?'

'No.'

'We were led to believe you were married.'

Mann hung his head for a second before looking back at Harry. 'I was. Yvonne died in a car crash years ago.'

'What did she do for a living?'

'She was a bus driver. She drove for Mike. She liked it because it was only along the road and she'd worked with him at the big bus company.'

'That must have been hard,' Dunbar said.

'It was. Still is. I only started driving because she introduced me to Mike. I had some debt and the extra money helped pay that off. Teachers aren't millionaires.'

'We have a witness who saw you bringing a young girl to the yard on your bus one night,' Stewart said.

Mann gave a little laugh. 'That's Denise. She's a teacher at Broomhouse High with me. We got chatting one day and started seeing each other. I miss my wife, but I have physical needs. Denise is small, but she's a thirty-one-year-old divorcee. She got my bus from the Gyle the other night because she'd been having dinner with a pal of hers at Frankie and Benny's. If you see Dougal Dixon again, you can tell him I saw his car was still in the yard that night he saw me with Denise.'

'He got it in for you, has he?'

'He just started hating the job. He didn't like me, although I had nothing against him. He told me Janice has a thing for me, and I believe him, as Janice has hinted that she'd like to go out sometime.'

'That's not what she told our colleague. She said

she comes along here for a bit of how's your father,'
Stewart said.

'What? Jesus. You have seen her, haven't you? I
have no intention of going out with her. I've had to
knock her back a few times. Denise told me that it was
an anonymous phone call that got me suspended. I
suspect it was Janice, being vindictive, but I can't prove
it. Yes, I talk to the students, but so do all the drivers.
We're just being friendly.'

'How does that work, you being a teacher then
going out driving a school bus?' Evans asked.

Mann looked puzzled. 'I don't drive the school bus.
When I say I talk to the students, I mean if they get on
the bus when they're going to the Gyle Centre or
something. It doesn't happen often, but occasionally I'll
see some of them. They say hello.'

'Who does the school bus run?'

'Mike does. He got that contract when he was
starting out and he still likes to do it now.'

'Were you doing a back shift two weeks ago on the
Saturday?' Dunbar said.

'No. I had the weekend off and I spent it with
Denise. She'll confirm that.' Mann fetched a piece of
paper and wrote her telephone number down. 'Call
her, ask her to confirm.'

'Do you have many guests here?' Dunbar said, not
taking his eyes off the man. 'Apart from Denise.'

'Sometimes we have friends round. But nobody from school. Students or otherwise. We like to have friends who aren't teachers.'

'Would you mind if we had a look around?' Stewart said, ready to add his spiel about getting a warrant.

'Not at all. Help yourselves. You have my permission to search anywhere in the house.'

'Thank you.'

'I just have to step outside for a moment. I have to speak to Mike and tell him I might be a wee bit late. Somebody can cover the first part of my shift.' Mann left the room and they saw him go out into the paved yard and stand near the garage, his phone to his ear.

'Let's get a move on. We don't want to go raking about in his drawers, but look for any signs of those lassies,' Stewart said.

They split up, Harry and Dunbar going through to the bedrooms and having a look around. When they were done searching, they went back to the living room and found Evans just finishing up.

'Fuck all,' Stewart declared. 'Except for three wine glasses on the wee drying rack by the sink, but that would hardly stand up in court. He might just be a lazy bastard who doesn't wash glasses until he has a pile going. No wonder he said we could look around.'

Mann came back in, smiling. 'Sorry about that.

Mike's going to get one of the other lads to do the first Clermiston for me.'

'Just one thing before you go,' Dunbar said. 'Have you ever seen' – *a monster or a ghost* – 'anybody creeping about the yard after dark?'

Mann shook his head. 'One driver thought he saw a ghost one night. Everybody took the piss, and he left after that. I don't think they knew my wife was a driver there and she died. They don't know she was also Mike's sister.'

'Thank you for your time, Mr Mann,' Stewart said, and they left.

Before Dunbar reversed out of the driveway, he looked at the others. 'Christ, he's either very convincing or very conniving. He could have gone out and called this Denise and told her to tell us a lot of shite, confirming his story.'

'I have an idea to see whether he was lying or not,' Stewart said. 'Get us back round to that yard.'

Dunbar got them back round in a minute, which was thirty seconds longer than it had taken before thanks to a white van shooting past.

'Stirling Moss there, for God's sake,' Stewart complained. 'Bloody white-van man indeed.'

The van indicated and turned into the yard, the unmarked car right behind it. They watched as it pulled up to the workshop garage where buses were fixed and a mechanic jumped out.

'A white van with no letters on the side,' Harry mused.

'Penny for them,' Stewart said.

'Nothing. Just thinking about that van, that's all. There was a white van down at Silverknowes when Abi was taken. The mother said a white van nearly took their door off.'

Dunbar parked in front of the office as a bus pulled out, presumably to cover Mann's shift, or the first part of it.

They walked into the canteen and found Janice sitting with yet another cup of tea. 'Bladder like an iron tank,' Lillian whispered to Harry as she got up.

Stewart stood towering over Janice. 'I'm going to ask you something and I want you to think about the answer very carefully before you speak. Bear in mind that I'm going to have a warrant for everybody here's phone records, yours included, so I'll know if you used your own phone to make the call. If it wasn't your mobile phone, I'll find out what one it was, then I'll make your life a living hell if you lie to me and I find out.'

Janice was holding a cup up to her mouth and was taking an inordinate amount of time to sip her tea, which looked like it could double as toilet cleaner.

'Did you make the anonymous phone call that caused Marshall Mann to be suspended from the school?'

Janice's eyes darted back and forth for a minute before she put the cup down slowly. 'I just wanted him to notice me, to maybe ask me out for a drink, get a bite to eat. But oh no, he threw himself at that Denise woman. How does she deserve to have all the fun?'

'Is that a yes?'

She nodded. 'Yes, it was me. I made it up.'

'You don't go round to his house for sex, do you?' Harry said.

She shook her head. 'No. Marshall is always a gentleman. So I lied, thinking he could spend more time here with me instead of with her. That's why I rushed out of here yesterday when you lot came in. I thought you were here to arrest me.'

'I could do you for obstructing a case,' Stewart said. 'But I won't if you call the school back and admit to them it was a hoax.'

'What will I tell them?'

Stewart shrugged. 'Tell them you're a jealous, bitter woman who should stay at home with her two cats.'

'How did you know I have two cats?'

'Just a guess,' he replied. 'Just a guess.'

THIRTY-SIX

'How's the search going for the wee lassie?' Stewart barked, all but knocking the door off its hinges as they stormed into the incident room.

Frank Miller looked at him. 'We're starting to get volunteers coordinated, sir. They're down at Silverknowes now, going to do a search for any sign of her. You know how these things go.'

'I do that, son, unfortunately.' Stewart looked at Evans. 'See if anybody else wants lunch. I'm Hank Marvin. And don't get KFC. That fuckin' car's honkin'.'

'How about a salad, sir?'

'Cheeky bastard. What are you trying to say? I'm a fat bastard like you?'

'Just trying to help you avoid having a pathologist cut you open at an early age.'

'Well, there goes my chances of wanting a hamburger. Just get me a chicken sandwich. Take the orders and get Lillian to go with you. It's on me. Or rather, Police Scotland.'

'That's very kind of you, sir.' Evans took a notepad and, with Lillian's help, took lunch orders.

The door opened and Muckle, Shug and Vern came in. Sparky got excited when he saw Stewart.

'Good boy. You showed that wee arsehole the other day, didn't you?' Stewart told them about the lunch order, but they'd already eaten.

'Fucking nash, and the drinks are on me tonight. Or Police Scotland, whatever way you want to look at it. But we need refreshments and you won't have to put your hand in your –'

Evans was gone before Stewart finished his sentence.

'Look at the wee bastard move when he wants to.'

Harry was talking to Miller and Eve Bell at a computer. He looked at Dunbar and Stewart. 'Says here that Mike Morton's sister was killed in a car crash six years ago. Not only that: her three kids died as well.'

'Does that have any bearing on the case?' Stewart asked.

'It might be nothing, but the kids were twelve, ten and eight when they died. Same ages as the first victims when they were taken. Same age as little Abi who just went missing.'

'But Ashley and Simone are older,' Eve Bell said.

'They're the ages Sandra Robertson and Alice Brent were when they were found,' Dunbar said.

Stewart walked away to Harry's office and went inside.

The incident room door opened and Alex Maxwell waddled in.

'Here she is, the lady of the moment,' Jimmy Dunbar said.

'Good to see you again, Alex.'

'It was only last night you saw me, Robbie,' she said.

'You know what Jimmy and Harry are like, a pair of comedians out of a bad sitcom. You're not here to keep them under control and they've lost the plot.'

'Don't worry, I'll be back soon.'

'Not that soon,' Harry said, coming up to her and smiling.

'It can't come soon enough.'

Lillian walked over, smiling. 'Hi, Alex. One day, when this case is finished, we should do lunch.'

'That would be nice.' Alex said it without any feeling.

'Good. I look forward to it.'

Stewart came back after a few minutes. 'Listen up,

folks.' He waited until he had everyone's attention. 'I just spoke to the procurator fiscal, outlining what we have on the investigation, and basically we have no grounds for a search warrant. Everything is speculation. If we find anything more concrete, then we can move forward.'

'We should tell that to Abi's parents,' Dunbar said.

'I know how you feel, Jimmy, but the decision is in the hands of the suits. We need to try that wee bit harder.'

'I have an idea,' Muckle McInsh said.

'Spit it out then, son,' Stewart said.

Muckle told him what he was thinking.

'That sounds good. Let's go with that.'

Eve Bell looked round from her computer. 'Sir?' she said to Harry.

He walked across to her desk and looked down at the computer screen. He looked up again after Eve pointed something out.

'Jimmy, sir, you might want to have a look at this before we finalise anything.'

THIRTY-SEVEN

As plans went, it wasn't much of one, but it was all they had. And time was running out for a little girl and two older girls who had been abducted, all of whom would be wanting to go home.

Technically, no passengers were allowed on the bus when it was returning to the yard, but on this occasion it stopped at the first stop in Turnhouse Road.

'How much is it for the dug to ride the bus, pal?' Muckle asked Marshall Mann.

'Sparky rides for free, my friend.'

'He likes free.' Muckle grinned as he took the dog on. Vern followed, and Wee Shug brought up the rear.

'I've never seen a real-life ghost,' Shug said as they sat down in the darkened single-decker bus. Mann drove along the road at normal speed.

'And you're not going to be seeing one now,' said Muckle. 'You do remember what the plan is, don't you?'

'Of course I do.'

'I forgot, this is past your bedtime. When the wee hand goes past twelve, you're always tucked up.'

'Actually, David and I sometimes play cards well into the wee hours.'

'Really?'

'Absolutely. Until one of us gets too blootered to carry on.'

'Dark horses and all that, eh, Vern?' Muckle said.

'Aye. Still waters.'

They were all dressed in black and could hardly be seen with all the interior lights off.

'Before we get to the yard, Marsh,' Muckle to Mann, 'let's have a quick rundown. In case spunky-baws is there.'

'Shoot.'

'How long have you known us?' Muckle asked.

'A year. We met at a car show in Glasgow. We became friends and our girlfriends became friends too.'

'My wife would kill me if she thought Vern was my girlfriend, but thank God this is only a story. And tonight we're what?'

'You came through to have dinner with me and

Denise. You took Sparky for a walk while the women were in the house, and I saw you waiting for me and gave you a lift along.'

'Great. That's all we need. The rest is all a phone call away.'

They went over the hump of the railway bridge, Walter Scott Travel's yard on the left, visible through the trees.

The bus slowed down to make the left into the Turnhouse Business Park. Mann slowed and they looked over at the old green house sitting forlornly in the dark. This place was poorly lit. The headlight beams cut through the darkness until they got to the yard, which was lit by one streetlight on the corner of the bus garage that bathed the yard in an orange glow.

'It's always the last door on the right, next to the office, so there's no guesswork as to where the bus should go,' Mann said.

'We'll follow your lead, pal.'

'I have to go and open the garage door from inside. I won't be a minute.' Mann stepped off the bus, and the three others and the dog got up and alighted into the cool night air.

Muckle looked around at the lights from the airport across the way, separated by a high chain-link fence. The workshop garage was over on the left, at ninety degrees to the main building, joined by a brick breeze-way. Where the 'monster' had appeared to Dougal Dixon, the ex-bus driver. The maintenance shed was on the right.

'I can imagine this might be a bit creepy if you came here on your own without a German Shepherd,' Shug said. 'Not for me, like,' he added.

'Of course not, Shug,' Vern said. 'Windowsills, yes; dark yards, no.' She grinned at him.

'You're just giving him ammunition, Vern.' Shug nodded to Muckle.

'You know I love you, Shug,' she said, putting her arm around him and smiling.

The garage door started clanking up electronically and the headlights from the bus lit the inside of the garage.

Marshall Mann wasn't there.

Muckle walked over to one side, Sparky on a short lead. 'Marsh?' he said, but there was no answer. Shug was by his side.

'Christ, look at that,' Vern said. She was looking at the green house in the distance, now looking black.

'What is it?' Muckle said, coming back out with Sparky. The dog, sensing something was up, started growling.

'Over there, at the house,' she said.

In an upstairs window there was the faintest light,

then a person came into view, dressed in what looked like a white gown and with long black hair.

'I'm going to check it out,' Vern said.

'Not on your own, Vern,' Muckle said.

'I'm just going to have a look. See where Marshall is and then come along.' She started walking back along the dark road, and soon she was swamped by the darkness and she appeared only as a dark shadow.

'He's gone,' Shug said, coming back out. 'Where's Vern?'

'Over there, in the dark. There's somebody in that house.'

'Who?'

'Well, we didn't sit down for tea and crumpets, but it looks like a fucking ghost.'

'Away. You're having me on.'

'Am I? Have a look for yourself.'

Shug looked at the house in the dark and saw the faint light with somebody standing in the window. Then the light went out and the person was no more.

'Fuck me. She shouldn't be going along there on her own.'

'I told her that, Shug, but she's a tough ex-copper who can handle herself.' Muckle turned to look back in the garage. 'Come on, let's have a neb in here. Marshall can't have disappeared.'

They walked forward to the open garage door in

front of the bus. Inside, other buses were parked up for the night, five in total. There was a door at the far end.

'He came in through the door on the right, came back here to press the button to lift the door, and then what?' Shug said.

'There's the door that leads through to the office. Check it out, Shug, and I'll check this door along here.'

'Aye-aye, Captain.' Shug walked along to the door, going in the opposite direction to Muckle. He tried the door handle and it turned. He looked round to tell Muckle, but the big man was already out of view round the front of the buses.

Shug stepped through and pulled his phone out, switching on the torch. The hallway turned left and he saw a door with the word *office* painted on it. The light reflected off the glass in the door. The handle was locked.

He carried on down the hallway and it turned a sharp right. Another hallway. A door faced him. He walked along, the light bouncing off the white walls. The hallway turned right again and there was another door. He tried the handle and it opened into the canteen.

He stepped inside and heard the low buzzing of two vending machines that spewed weak light into the room, barely illuminating the tables and chairs. There was a door over on the right and a quick look showed him the maintenance workshop.

He turned back to the room and saw another door tucked away in the corner.

Shug walked towards it.

THIRTY-EIGHT

'Sparks, play the fucking game. There's grease or oil on the floor here, pal. You nearly had me on my arse again.'

Sparky pulled him round the corner to a door. Muckle got him to sit while he opened it. There was the brick breezeway he had seen from the outside. Had Marshall come along here? Muckle walked along and opened the door at the far end. It opened into another, smaller workshop. There were tools in here and a garage door over on the left.

There was no sign of Marshall, so Muckle about-turned and walked back the way he had come. The bus's headlights were still illuminating the garage entrance as it sat outside.

He crossed over the bay and went through the door that Shug had gone through, taking out a small torch.

He followed the hallway round and went into the canteen. He checked the maintenance workshop, but it was empty.

He swung the torch about. 'Shug?' he said, without actually shouting it.

Nothing.

He walked over to what looked like a steel door, but it didn't have a handle on it.

Shug was nowhere to be seen. Had he nipped out the open garage door where the bus was waiting? No, he wouldn't do that, not without telling Muckle.

Another sweep of the room and all he saw was the two vending machines.

His torchlight caught something lying on the floor.

A half-eaten chocolate bar.

Shug was gone.

Muckle turned and made his way back to the garage bay, switched his torch off and started sprinting along to the dark house at the end of the road.

Sparky sensed something was up but didn't start barking. He stopped for a second and sniffed the ground. Muckle was sure the dog had picked up Vern's scent.

He moved again and Muckle started running faster. This had been his plan and it was all going down the toilet.

THIRTY-NINE

The green house still looked black as Vern got up close to it. She supposed there had to have been a reason the RAF had chosen this olive colour. The colour of it wasn't at the forefront of her mind, though, as she kept close to the walls.

It was how to get in.

The windows and doors had been boarded up and nature was slowly clawing its way back, covering some of the windows with trees and bushes. A wind was blowing off the airport, shaking the trees.

She walked round the perimeter, her eyes adjusting to the darkness. She walked clockwise, figuring there was less chance of being seen from the airport side than there was from the road, although the traffic was very light.

She rounded the corner and approached the back

of the house. She wondered what this had been, back in the Spitfire days. Further back, the old control tower sat at the front of some more old buildings.

Then she saw it: a loose board that was covering a door and was now hanging to one side. Not obvious if you were driving by this side but obvious close up.

She pulled it away a little bit further and slipped inside. She took out a small torch and shone it around. She saw a hallway in front of her. Paint was peeling like dead skin and some detritus was lying on the floor. Old newspapers and rubbish. It smelled musty and old, like it was a museum dedicated to the squadrons who had served here for years.

She thought she heard a noise upstairs and walked along as quietly as she could.

There it was again. She realised she was holding her breath as she walked along the hallway. It opened into a main hallway at the entrance to the house, with stairs to her left. She slowly looked round for any sign of the light she had seen at the window, but there was nothing.

She walked past the stairs and saw a door on the other side, leading down to what she assumed was a basement. It was slightly open. She thought she could see a faint glow, but then it was pitch black again.

Then she heard a sound behind her, rushing along the hallway she'd just come along, and she took her baton and flicked it open and held it above her shoulder.

Then she heard a familiar sound.

'Jesus Christ, Sparky, I nearly peed myself there,' she said as the dog rushed at her, wagging his tail.

'Shug's gone,' Muckle said in a whisper. 'He and Mann have both disappeared. I looked in the bus garage, but there was no sign of him. The only thing I saw was a half-eaten chocolate bar still in its wrapper.'

'Where do you think they went?'

Suddenly, a light came on downstairs.

FORTY

'Are you okay?' Harry asked Denise. The woman looked ashen, like all the blood had evaporated from her body.

'I'm scared.'

'It's going to be alright,' Dunbar said. 'These officers here are going to escort you to a safe house, just for the time being.' He nodded towards Eve Bell and Karen Shiels. 'Two other officers are waiting outside for you. That's four members of my team who I would trust with my life. Nobody is going to come near you, especially Marshall Mann.'

'Thank you.' She had stopped crying, but shock had set in. 'Are you sure about all of this? There's no room for error? Maybe a mistake was made?'

Harry could see the hope in her eyes, the faintest

glimmer that she was holding on to. She was waiting for words of comfort that weren't going to come.

'I'm sorry, there's no mistake. It was double-checked, and we had a computer expert run over the details and he was able to confirm what we thought. The man you moved in with isn't what you thought he was. But let me ask you one thing: he said you rode the bus back to the garage with him at the end of a shift recently. And you were standing on the bus kissing him. Is that true?'

She shook her head. 'No, I wasn't on his bus.'

Harry knew then that what Dougal Dixon had witnessed was Mann taking a young girl back to the garage to have sex with her.

Denise left with the officers, then Harry, Dunbar and Stewart went through the door and down the stairs.

'I thought these bastard things had lights in them,' Calvin Stewart said as they walked along the tunnel, their torchlight bouncing off the walls. Pipes and conduits were high up and seemed to go on forever.

'They do, but we can't switch them on,' Dunbar said in a tone that was normally reserved for somebody who was drunk and couldn't understand why it was so difficult to get his trousers off.

'I haven't done this much walking since...well,

maybe at Tulliallan. Not outside anyway. I walk on a treadmill at home. What about you, Harry? You a street or treadmill man?'

'Street. I like the fresh air.'

'I like to watch Netflix while I'm on my treadmill, and I can still walk when it's pishing down outside. What about you, Jimmy?'

'Do I look like I exercise?'

'You do, actually. Skinny bastard. You make me fucking sick at times. Here's me and Harry having to sweat like a pair of bastards to keep the weight off, while you eat all the shite under the sun and stay like a beanpole.'

'I thought you said the doc told you that you have the metabolism of a furnace?'

'I did. He did. But I still have to keep myself healthy. Especially now, since my wife fucked off. I'm thinking of going on that dating site – what's it called again? Kindling or something.'

'Tinder.'

'Aye, I knew it had something to do with fire.'

'As long as your baws don't feel like they're on fire after you've been out with some wee hoor,' Harry said.

'Thanks for that image, there.'

The three men were speed-walking and their breaths were coming fast, and just as Harry was about to think there was no end to this tunnel, it opened up into a small room. There were panels on one wall. And a steel door. It looked old, with paint chipping off it.

'If this doesn't open, we're fucked,' Stewart said.

It opened.

FORTY-ONE

Vern's phone vibrated in her pocket. She took it out and read the text. 'It's from Robbie,' she whispered. 'He's there now. Lillian's with him, but he's going to need help. Things are moving fast.'

'Let's get a move on then. If what we think happened did happen, then it's going to end tonight.'

Muckle looked down the stairs into the basement at the faint light and started making his way down, keeping Sparky on a very tight lead. At the bottom, a wooden door stood open. Inside was a false shelving unit that had been pushed to one side, revealing a steel door. That too was open.

They stepped through the door and into a hallway and could see the light was coming from round the corner. Muckle walked forward, still keeping Sparky on a short lead. The dog growled.

'Easy, boy,' he whispered.

They walked round the corner and saw a couple of dim bulbs lighting the hallway and pipes high up on the wall.

The hallway turned left and then they were in a larger hallway. Several doors led off this and Muckle looked through a doorway. There was a large room, but he could only see as far as the shaft of light from the open door would allow. He stood on the threshold and suddenly the lights came on in the room.

Shug was sitting on the floor, his hands behind his back, presumably tied, his mouth gagged with a cloth.

There were steel beds lined up against a wall, and some steel lockers formed a wall facing him. Muckle felt his heart beat faster.

Sparky started growling as Mike Morton stepped out from behind the lockers, holding a shotgun.

'That's it, son, keep the dog under control, or I'll shoot it.'

'You shoot my dog, I'll kill you afterwards.'

'Oh dear, I was afraid this was going to happen.' Morton pointed the shotgun at Shug's head. 'Both of you, come further into the room, or the first cartridge will kill your friend. And I have plenty of ammo.'

Muckle hesitated. He heard shoes scraping the concrete floor behind him. He and Vern turned to look.

'You need to listen to him,' Marshall Mann said.

They moved further into the room, towards their friend.

'Why couldn't you three have minded your own business?' Mann said.

Vern walked over to Shug. Morton pointed the gun at her, but she ignored him and took the gag out of Shug's mouth.

'He's not a bloody animal, for God's sake.'

Morton laughed. 'It doesn't matter now. It was only to stop him alerting you.'

'The place is well alight. It's going to be an inferno shortly. I set the fire along the corridor,' another voice said from outside the room. Agnes Morton stepped in. 'He's right; you should have minded your own business.'

'What was all that shite you told McNeil?' Muckle asked. 'Your wife died and you met Denise and she's moving in with you and you don't look at school lassies. Isn't that what you told him?'

Mann laughed. 'I did. And I thought he fell for it. Obviously not, though.'

'I think the news article about your kids dying and your wife surviving might have had something to do with it,' Vern said.

'You told him that?' Morton said to Mann.

'No. I just said my wife died years ago. I didn't go into details. Who cares? This place is going to go up like a bonfire now that we've switched the sprinklers off.'

'What is this place?' Shug asked.

'It's a nuclear bunker,' Morton said.

'Where are the kids?'.

'Safe. For now,' Agnes answered.

'Did the three of you kill those other girls?' Muckle said.

'It was an accident,' Mann replied. 'That's the God's honest truth.'

'Was it?' Muckle looked at Agnes. 'Why don't you ask *him* about it?' He nodded to her husband.

'What does he mean?' said Agnes.

'Nothing. He's playing games with us,' Morton answered, but Agnes and Mann were watching him.

'What? I tried fixing the boiler and something went wrong. They died of carbon monoxide poisoning and we kept them in the big freezer. You both know all of that. We had to get rid of them. For *his* wife. *My* sister.'

'The wife who isn't dead,' Muckle said, still keeping a tight hand on his dog.

'That's right. My kids died in the car crash,' said Mann. 'My wife, Mike's sister, she's the one who survived, but she was mentally broken and half her face was burnt off. She needed taking care of, so we decided to let her live down here. She has absolutely everything she would have up in the real world. Except her freedom to go about. We missed the girls so much.'

'So you replaced them with three new ones,' Vern said. 'Let me guess; those girls were the same age as your own children when they died.'

'They were. They got used to living here. They were my family. I told them at first that if they left, I'd kill their own family. They got used to being around us after a while.'

'Until Mike here killed them,' Muckle said.

'I told you it was an accident,' Morton said, getting agitated.

'Really? Or was it getting rid of the evidence? Easy enough to tamper with the boiler in that room. Did you tell your wife that Sandra was pregnant?'

'What? You're a liar,' Agnes said. 'Sandra wasn't pregnant.'

'That's not what the pathologist told us. Three months. It was time for her to go, so nobody would find out he was interfering with them. Is that why you took Ashley and Simone? So you would have older ones right away to assault, instead of having to wait years again?'

'Don't listen to him,' Morton said.

'Is it true?' Agnes asked him, stepping closer.

Tendrils of smoke began to enter the room.

'I asked you if it's true!' she shouted at her husband.

He started crying. 'I was weak. I couldn't help it.'

She looked at him for a moment. 'Give me the gun.'

He sniffed and looked at her. 'What?'

'Give me the gun.'

He handed it over. 'What are you going to do?'

'I'm going to take the girls. Start a new life.'

'No, please! Let me have Ashley. She's seventeen.'

Agnes sucked in a breath and pulled the trigger, blowing a hole in her husband's chest. She swung the gun round as Sparky went into a rage.

'Keep back. I have more ammo. I will kill you all.' She circled round them and headed for another doorway, then stopped at the threshold. 'Get out of here, Marshall. Run. You know the way; they don't!' She stepped through and slammed the door shut.

Mann turned to the other door, about to do the same and lock them in.

Muckle slipped Sparky's lead off. 'Radge!' he shouted.

The dog flew at Mann, grabbing his arm. He fell as Muckle and Vern rushed forward, but Mann managed to kick the door shut. There was no handle on the inside.

'Sparky!' Muckle shouted, utter panic gripping him now.

'Open doors, does he?' Mann shouted from outside the door, then they heard a scream.

Then the door opened.

Harry McNeil was standing there.

As was Mann's wife, dressed in her white gown. She was holding a large knife, blood dripping from it. Blood was pouring from Mann's mouth.

'Sparky! Leave!' Muckle shouted, and the dog sensed there was no more threat and let Mann go.

His wife dropped the knife and looked at Harry, before turning and running back to where the flames were licking round the corner and the smoke was getting thicker.

Muckle rubbed Sparky and clipped his lead back on.

'We need to get the hell out of here,' Harry said as Vern untied Shug.

'The exit's blocked by the fire!' Muckle shouted.

'That one is. The other one's not. The one Jimmy and Stewart took. And Agnes Morton.'

They started running.

FORTY-TWO

There was something different about Ashley. What had they been doing down there? Agnes Morton thought as she slowly walked into her kitchen. Her breaths were still coming fast, but it was under control. Ashley was standing at the sink.

It's time for you to go, Agnes thought, putting the shotgun down. *I wish things could have ended better.* She had a short piece of rope in her hand. She knew she could never start over again with the girls. They would hunt them down. It would be a massive manhunt. Better they all go together.

She stepped forward, lifting the rope, and Lillian O'Shea turned round, putting up a hand, and grabbed the rope.

'Ashley's safe. They all are,' she said as Robbie

Evans grabbed Agnes from behind and threw her on the floor.

Jimmy Dunbar and Calvin Stewart burst in, followed by what seemed like hundreds of uniforms.

'We saw her running along in front of us,' said Dunbar. 'Harry diverted. We followed her up through that secret door in the garage.'

'Did you see Vern?' Evans asked, a worried look on his face.

'No, son. Smoke was starting to pour out and we can see the house is on fire now.'

'Jesus.' Evans pulled his phone out and dialled Vern's number. 'Oh God, I was worried.' He looked at Dunbar. 'They're all out.'

'Thank Christ for that,' Dunbar said. He went outside to wait for them. It was starting to rain when they got there, five minutes later.

'Fire brigade's on their way. The airport lot too,' Harry said. 'We got well away in case something goes up.'

'Agnes Morton is being taken away now. That was nice timing, seeing her running out of there. She led us right here. Thank Christ we had those blueprints or else we would have got lost coming from Mann's house.'

'You're not out of breath, are you, Jimmy?' Vern said.

'Don't you start. I'll hear enough of it from Robbie.'

Evans came out and Sparky wanted attention first. Evans petted him before giving Vern a hug.

'Where's my hug?' Stewart said, coming out. Evans let Vern go and turned to the boss. 'Touch me and I'll rip your fucking bollocks off.' He sidestepped Evans, who just shrugged, and Stewart hugged Vern. 'Good job.'

'Thank you, sir.'

'Now we just have to come up with a report for the procurator fiscal,' Harry said. 'But we should go and interview Agnes Morton first.'

Harry stood next to one of the multiple police vehicles strewn across the road, their blue lights flashing. He took his phone out and dialled a number.

'Hi. I figured you'd still be up. I just wanted to tell you I love you.'

'I love you too, Harry McNeil. Did you complete the job?' Alex asked.

'We did. It went almost according to plan. But we have to get Agnes Morton booked in and interviewed. I'll be a while yet.'

'I'll be here.'

FORTY-THREE

There was no arrogance about her, like Harry had thought there would be. Big, tough Agnes Morton, child killer. Now, sitting across from him and Jimmy Dunbar, she just seemed like a shrivelled-up little woman.

She knew she was being recorded, but none of it mattered anymore.

'Everything was ticking along nicely,' she said. She was wrapped in a blanket because she felt cold inside. Her hands were wrapped round a hot cup of tea. 'We were one big happy family. Until the day Marshall decided that he needed Yvonne to drive the kids to the beach. She hadn't been feeling well, like a cold was coming on, and she'd taken cold medicine that made her drowsy. But Marshall had his eyes on a seventeen year old he'd met. He told Mike that later. So Yvonne drove and fell asleep at the wheel. She lost control, the car burst into flames and she had half her face burnt. The kids died.'

'They were twelve, ten and eight years old at the time?' Dunbar asked.

'Yes. After she got out of hospital, Yvonne couldn't face the world. And they lived in that little cottage, so it wasn't as if she had neighbours next door to help. She didn't go out at all. Ever. She wanted to die. Then one day, she went walking in the tunnels under the house. The RAF had a bunker under the green house in the business park, from back in the day when it was an RAF base. She knew about it, and the tunnel that led to their house was a fire escape. She lived there alone before she met Marshall. After the crash, she moved down into the bunker. It was like a huge house underground with everything she needed. She wanted to stay where people couldn't see her hideous features. So we let her. And told other people she had died with the kids in a car crash. Mike and I knew there was a fire escape tunnel that led from the green house to our garage. Mike's parents left him that house, and Yvonne got the cottage. Their father told them about the bunker and the tunnels.'

'She lived there all the time?' Harry said. 'In the bunker?' It was after two in the morning and he felt he should have been tired, but he was wired instead.

'Yes. She felt safe, but she was missing the kids. So we decided to do something about it.'

'We, meaning?' Dunbar asked.

'Me, Mike and Marshall. We had no intention of ever hurting the kids. We didn't know how to abduct children, or who to take, then Mike thought about the drivers who had daughters. And the mechanic. It was easy after that. They went to the school I taught at. Three of them at the same school. Who would have thought?'

Harry felt sick to his stomach. Sitting across from this monster.

'Then what?' he said.

'They knew Marshall too, of course. He approached Sandra at Portobello, got talking to her – asking her for help or something; I can't quite remember. I had the minibus waiting. We took her. And little Alice Brent. I slipped away from my class, who were just about ready to come out, and I waved Alice over in the car park of the leisure centre.'

'You didn't have a dog with you?' Dunbar asked, thinking of Vern's reasoning that the abductor might have had a dog with him.

'No. I told her a friend of mine had one with her, though, and it had slipped off the lead. Marshall was waiting with the minibus and he took her away. She went willingly.'

'And Zoe Harris, who went missing in Burntisland?' Harry asked.

'She was running about. Don't let her parents fool you when they tell you they kept their eyes on her. They weren't paying attention at all. I met her, and Mike was waiting with the minibus. She came willingly too. Then we had three kids who were the same age as Marshall's when they died.'

'And they lived happily ever after.'

'There were some extreme times, but after a couple of years, they settled down. They came out at night. We helped, but sometimes Yvonne would bring them up, and once or twice a driver spotted something. There was rumours going about that the place was haunted. Nobody believed anything.'

'Then they died?' Dunbar said.

'Yes. I thought it was an accident, but you said Mike got Sandra pregnant and how could that be explained away? Dirty bastard. I never knew he was touching them. He was always going down to help. He fixed the boiler in that room but he obviously tampered with it. He said he'd accidentally killed them, so he put them in the walk-in freezer until he figured out what to do with them. He wanted to put them back where they were taken from, to try and throw the police off the scent. To confuse you lot. Fat lot of good that did.'

'Why did he take Ashley and Simone?' Harry asked.

'He thought he was just replacing Sandra and Alice, but now I think he wanted them older so he could have sex with them. I complained about taking older girls, and he took little Abi. He was at Silverknowes with the service van and he got her away from her friends and told her that he had a puppy.'

'And you were quite happy with that?' Dunbar said.

'It was for Yvonne.'

'You went up to take the girls, but you had a rope. You were going to strangle Ashley,' Harry said. 'Only it wasn't Ashley.'

'I knew I wouldn't get away. When I was running from you, I thought it would be better to end it for us all. I didn't realise it was one of your officers there.'

'Were any of the parents involved?' Harry asked.

Agnes shook her head. 'No. None of them.'

After a few more questions, they had her taken away by uniforms.

'At least some families get their kids back,' Dunbar said.

'Aye. Silver linings.'

FORTY-FOUR

They were the last ones in the dining room. It was the older woman who was on duty again, and she was only too pleased to accommodate them all. An extra twenty let Sparky lie in the corner.

'Here, hen –' Stewart said, but the woman just smiled.

'I already got him to do extra tattie scones.'

'Ye're a doll. You'll be looked after, sweetheart.' Stewart looked at Lillian and Vern. 'What? I'm old. I can get away with calling a woman sweetheart. I draw the line at you two, though. I wouldn't want to be written up.'

'Like you could care,' Dunbar said.

'Oh, I forgot,' Stewart said, reaching into his inside pocket. He brought an envelope out and handed it to Harry. 'Add something to the pot. We all chipped in for Katie for putting up with us all. There's over a hundred quid there. Make it swell.'

Harry took his wallet out and added to it, very generously.

'Here's your coffee, sir,' Evans said, putting the mug down.

'You must be after a promotion or something.'

'Not at all, sir. Just being helpful.'

'Lying wee sod,' Stewart replied in a low voice.

'I'm no' deef,' Evans said.

'You were meant to hear that.'

Alex came in. 'I feel a fraud, coming over here for breakfast when I didn't work the case.'

'Don't be daft. I'll get you a chair,' Stewart said. 'Evans! Get the lady a chair.'

Evans turned round from the coffee station and rushed over with a chair for Alex.

'Thanks, Robbie,' she said, smiling at him.

He winked at her.

'Right, now we all have a drink, let's celebrate getting those lassies back. And pay our respects to those who didn't come home.'

They all raised their coffee mugs.

They ate breakfast and swapped stories until it was time to leave.

'We're going to come through and wet the baby's head,' Dunbar said. 'Eh, Robbie?'

'I'll be there.'

'Me too,' Muckle said. 'Sparky will stay home with my wife.'

'I'll be there, Harry,' Shug said.

'Good man,' Harry said.

Stewart was looking down at his plate.

'You too, sir?' Harry said.

Stewart looked up. 'You want me there?'

'Of course I do. The more the merrier.'

'Magic! If you come through to Glasgow for it, I know some great fucking strip clubs.'

Alex looked at him.

'I'm kidding. We will, of course, be through here.'

They said their goodbyes and Alex walked out with Harry. Following them was Lillian.

'If you're going to have a girls' night out, I can help you arrange it, if you like.'

Alex looked at her for a moment, thinking back to when she first started on the force and was abandoned by her friends. How she was treated like crap by a former boss and had to stand up for herself. With no best friend by her side.

Alex slipped an arm through Lillian's and smiled at her. 'Come round to ours and I'll get the kettle on. I'd like to hear your ideas.'

AFTERWORD

Being a writer means we get to have fun with real places and twist the facts a little to suit our own ends, so the story slots together just that little bit tighter. So I played around with some places in Edinburgh. Just so nobody could say, *Hey, I don't like you using that name*, etc.

North Merchiston Primary School doesn't exist. I made it up for the sake of the book.

Turnhouse Business Park existed, but I changed the buildings just a tad. The bus garage did exist, as did the maintenance shed next to it, and the little workshop/garage. The green house did exist. There once was a bunker in there somewhere. I don't know how far it went or what was down there, but RAF Turnhouse did have a bunker.

Being from Edinburgh and now living in New

York, I have to use Google Street View quite a bit. If you look at the latest photos of the Turnhouse Business Park on Turnhouse Road, you'll see the buildings have been demolished. But if you're on a computer, look at the box in the top-left corner, click on the 'street view' button and look at 2008. You'll see the green house on the right, just inside the main gates.

The cottage where Marshall Mann lived does exist, but I think it's two cottages. I don't know if there is a tunnel underneath.

Schools do exist at the location in South Gyle, but the names Broomhouse High and St. Francis High are fictitious. Not sure about now, but a long time ago the kids did get onto school buses at South Gyle Broadway.

I want to stress that this book is not based on any real-life case. I used the Portobello location because it was a place I went to many times over the years.

I would like to thank my wife and daughters as usual, and also my advance reading team, who are just fantastic. A big thank you to Jacqueline Beard, Ruth from Police Scotland and Anne Strang.

And an enormous thank you to Charlie Wilson, who stepped in and made a really difficult time that little bit easier. You don't know how much that means to me.

Also thank you to the Carson family. I love you all.

Thank you to my readers, who make this all worthwhile.

Just one thing before you go – if I could please ask you to leave a review or a rating on Amazon or Goodreads, that would really help me out. Each one is truly appreciated.

All the best, my friends,

John Carson
New York
April 2021

ABOUT THE AUTHOR

John Carson is originally from Edinburgh but now lives with his wife and family in New York State. He shares his house with four cats and two dogs.

website - johncarsonauthor.com
    Facebook - JohnCarsonAuthor
    Twitter - JohnCarsonBooks
    Instagram - JohnCarsonAuthor